# ONLY A
# PRAYER AWAY

*Gaetano J. Burtone*

**FriesenPress**

Suite 300 – 990 Fort Street
Victoria, BC, Canada V8V 3K2
www.friesenpress.com

**ISBN**
978-1-4602-5253-6 (Hardcover)
978-1-4602-5254-3 (Paperback)
978-1-4602-5255-0 (eBook)

1. Fiction, Coming Of Age

Photo of author taken by Steven Lorenz.

Distributed to the trade by The Ingram Book Company

# TABLE OF CONTENTS

For Carmela, Brianna, and Michael.
You have been the answers to all my prayers.

For my Dad, I hope you are proud of me. I miss you.

# ACKNOWLEDGMENTS

I SPENT MANY HOURS ALONE IN THE WRITING OF THIS story. This might give you the impression that this was completely an individual effort. It was not. Every person's life is like a book. There is a beginning, middle, and an end, but most important are the people who grace the pages of your life. Without the pages, the book is empty. I want to say thank you to all of you who have added to the pages of my life.

If you read this story and we know each other, I hope this story brings us closer. If you read this story and we don't know each other, well then I hope this can be the start of a new friendship.

To my family: Mom, Joe, Dee, Dawn, Bob, Abigail and James. I love you. My life is blessed because of all of you.

To all of my friends and family: Thank you so much for all of the great times that we have spent together. I also want to thank you for all the times that we comforted each other when life was difficult.

To John (Duke), Andy (Chew), Tommy (Pheeno), Steve (Ogs) and Tony (Jaws): I am forever grateful for the childhood we spent together.

Tony C: I still think of you.

To all the people at FriesenPress: I want to thank all of you for your support during this process. It was wonderful working with you.

Prayer is a wonderful power placed by Almighty God in the hands of His saints, which may be used to accomplish great purposes and to achieve unusual results. Prayer reaches to everything, takes in all things great and small which are promised by God to men. The only limit to prayer, are the promises of God and His ability to fulfill those promises.

The Possibilities of Prayer
E.M. Bounds

"Men ought always to pray"
Luke 18:1, KJV

# PROLOGUE

# CHRISTMAS EVE 2002

A HEAVY SNOW FALLS, TURNING THE STREETS WHITE. Colorful Christmas lights adorn the houses, and reflect brightly against the snow. A car rolls by silently, the sound of its engine muffled by the blanket of snow covering the streets. I walk alone through the streets of the neighborhood of my youth, thinking back to Christmas Eve twenty-five years ago. The memories, still fresh, run through my mind. That was the Christmas that changed everything. That was the Christmas that led me here, alone in the snow, looking for answers so many years later.

Christmas Eve is a night to be home with loved ones. A night to reflect and be grateful, and as much as I want to be home, there are no answers for me there. I pass a house from my childhood, which spurs a new flood of memories. Wanting to feel the warmth and peace of Christmas, I look through the front window and recognize the family inside. Under normal circumstances I would stop in to say hello, share a drink, and exchange holiday wishes. Not tonight. Tonight there is no warmth or peace, only the cold that comes from fear—of not knowing what tomorrow may bring.

My thoughts blur as my walk continues, and before long I find myself in front of the church I attended as a young boy. I spent many moments in this church. More memories flood back. Entering the church, the warmth embraces me and I leave the cold winter night behind. The sound of a Christmas carol, sung by young, heavenly voices, fills the air. I walk down the aisle unnoticed, kneel down, cross myself, and enter a pew.

I pay little attention to the song as it continues, admiring instead the stained glass windows that circle the church, depicting the twelve stations of the cross. The song ends. A new one begins: "Oh Holy Night". The softness of the voices comforts me as I close my eyes. When I open them, they fall upon a pretty red-haired girl in the choir. She's no more than ten years old and has a smile bright enough to light up a dark room. I watch her as she sings, and follow her eyes, which lead me to a man and a woman huddled together in a front pew. From their proud expressions, I assume they're her parents. Something inside me stirs as I watch the three of them, and I know that tonight (Christmas Eve) is just about that—about the love that exists between a parent and a child. It's what brought me to the church tonight. It's what makes me still think about that Christmas so long ago, and reminds me that some memories never really fade away.

I stand to leave and say a silent prayer as the choir continues its melodic hymns. I glance back at the young and innocent little girl and find myself hoping that she knows how much her parents love her.

As I leave the warmth and comfort of the church, the cold and the snow greet me once more. I walk a short distance and then suddenly turn back. My eyes focus on the large cross that sits atop the church, and somewhere inside me stirs a hope that the answer to all my fears hangs on that cross. I find myself wishing that, tonight, it will offer me hope. Maybe my only hope.

I continue to walk slowly, the only sound, the crunch of pristine snow beneath my feet. I walk until I find myself looking at the house in which I grew up, my heart growing heavy again. Inside, my family is gathered for the holiday. The house is happy but subdued compared to others on the street, and as my eyes move from house to house, I recall distinct and happy times spent in each of them during my childhood.

Yet the pain in my heart continues. I look towards my parents' home once again, hoping to gain some measure of comfort. There is none.

I gaze upward and admire the gently falling snow, and once again question the events of the day. My eyes shift back to my parents' house and my mind races back to that time, twenty-five years ago—to when this story really began.

I look up to the sky and whisper:

"Not again. Please God. Not again."

# Chapter 1

# Family

My name is Michael Parisi and I grew up in Staten Island, New York, with my dad, Anthony, my mom, Barbara, my brother, David, my sister, Jackie, and tons of friends and relatives.

My parents were like many of the adults in my neighborhood. Most had come from either Brooklyn or Manhattan, looking to give their children a better life than they'd had. They met when they were in high school, dated, and then married. Dad was drafted into the army and my mom worked as a legal secretary in Manhattan. I was born in 1964, my brother in 1967, and my 'baby' sister in 1970.

My parents were the children of immigrants who had left their homeland in search of a better life. Because of this, there was a deep appreciation of the life that was afforded them in America—an appreciation handed down to their children. They never forgot what life was like in their homeland, and often told stories of growing up in Italy and of the hard times they'd endured. My parents often recounted these stories to us so that we would also grow up with an appreciation of what America afforded us, and an appreciation of where our family came from. And we did appreciate it. All of it.

Religion was a constant in our lives. We were Roman Catholic and so was everyone in our town. Our lives revolved around the church. We went to school there, played on sports teams in the Catholic Youth Organization (CYO), and went to confession as often as needed. The walls of our house were covered with pictures of Jesus and various saints. Each of the saints had a special meaning or prayer that was applicable to someone in the family. I didn't really mind, but my mom had this rule that when you entered a room that had a picture of Jesus in it, you had to cross yourself...*every time* you entered the room. And if you forgot, she reminded you...every time.

My father was a big man, probably about six foot four. He had a large, barrel chest, big hands, and a round friendly face that was full of expression. He may have been physically imposing but he was really just a gentle soul. He was strict, but never hit us, and was extremely affectionate. After a three-year stint in the army, he returned home and joined the New York City Police Department.

Dad was not a big talker, but when he spoke, you listened. He taught me many life lessons, most of which I still remember today. One in particular stays with me:

"Home is where you should always want to be; if you have a bad day at work, or life is getting you down, home is where you should want to be. A man who is happy at home is always a rich man."

Not bad for a guy who never had the chance to go to college.

Mom was small, maybe five foot two, with an angular face that turned bright as the sun when she smiled. She was not at all physically imposing, but she possessed an inner toughness and strength that I haven't seen in many other people. She was very tough with us, but very loving. She had a lot of rules and she didn't compromise on any of them. She was actually tougher than my father, but she filled all of our lives with love and did more for me than anyone ever has. Like most of the women in our town, she stopped working when her children were born and became a full-time mother.

The other great thing about my mother was that she always loved having people around. She was more outgoing than my father and our house was always full with family and friends. If I was out with my friends during a summer day, we inevitably wound up back at our house for some lunch and then swimming in the pool. My friends all agreed that my mom made the best lunches, and always made you feel like you were home.

I will always be grateful for her warmth, and how she always told us to never be afraid. "Work hard and trust in God and you will be okay," she said, more times than I can remember.

Mom had four sisters and a brother, and they all lived near us. Dad had a brother named Rich, and a sister named Connie. They also lived nearby. I was extremely close to the both of them.

Uncle Rich was a cool guy. He was educated—the first person in the family to graduate from college. He had a professional job, traveled, wore really nice clothes, and was single. All the men that I knew were married. Uncle Rich was the only single man I knew. It seemed like, every holiday, he showed up with a different woman. They were always young, pretty, and quiet. All the women I knew were always yelling, at either their kids or their husbands! Being single seemed pretty cool to me. If things started getting crazy with a girl, you could just go look for another!

It was Uncle Rich who bought me my first baseball glove, and took me to my first baseball game at Yankee Stadium. He told me stories of all his travels, and always brought me something back from the places he had been. He always had time for me. He wasn't my dad, but I loved him as much as I could love anyone who wasn't, and although I couldn't put it into words when I was young, I always felt that we were joined to each other in some way—that our lives shared a common purpose. He was, and still is, one of my heroes.

After my grandmother died, Aunt Connie became the "head" of the family. The perception by outsiders is that the men rule the house in an Italian family. All Italians know that this isn't quite true. The families are ruled by women of character, decency, and with the capacity to spread equal amounts of love and guilt. When she spoke, everyone listened. We loved her, but we were also a little afraid of her—even Dad and the other men in the family.

I remember one occasion my father, Uncle Rich, and Uncle Paul were sitting comfortably in the den at Aunt Connie's house watching football. Uncle Frank, who had just arrived, walked into the room and announced that dinner was ready. The men responded to this announcement by glancing at each other, mumbling a few words, and then very slowly starting to get up. As Uncle Frank walked out of the room, Aunt Connie stormed in. She looked around and announced, "Dinner is ready now, guys!"

"Here we go," Dad said, as he stood up quickly.

"Coming!" Uncle Rich responded, trying not to be noticed by Connie.

Uncle Paul moved quickly towards the TV, "I'll get the TV!"

They all vacated the room in no time.

Aunt Connie was married and had four children, but the bond she had with my dad and Uncle Rich was really amazing. Their father had died when they were all young, and their mother was forced to go to work to support them. Because of this, they spent many hours and even whole days alone with each other. They learned to need and trust each other in a way that can only be forged by desperation. My dad would tell me stories of how Aunt Connie would take care of him and Uncle Rich when their mother wasn't around.

There was one story that I always remember:

Shortly after his father's death, Dad and his family moved to a small house in Brooklyn. One day, when he was about seven years old, he did not feel well at all.

"Mom? Mom! Where are you? Mom, I don't feel good! My stomach hurts and my head too!" My grandmother came into his room, sat down on his bed, and put her lips to his forehead. "You're a little warm, but no fever," she said. "You should stay home today. You probably have a virus, but I really have to go to work, sweetie. Now just lie in bed and drink plenty of water, and I'll be home before you know it." With that, she was gone and Aunt Connie and Uncle Rich left for school.

My father was sick, frightened, and home alone for the first time.

Later that morning, as he lay in bed crying, he heard the front door open. "She's home!" he said out loud, thinking, of course, that it was his mother. But it was his sister instead. Connie had snuck out of school to come home and take care of him. She held him tight as he cried in her arms. She calmed him down, made him a hot cup of tea, some toast, and gently washed his face with a cool rag. She held him until he fell asleep.

My dad told me this story many times, and every time he did, his eyes filled with tears.

When I think of that story, and others like it, I realize that even some blood bonds are thicker than others.

# CHAPTER 2

# NEIGHBORHOOD

ALONG WITH YOUR FAMILY AND FRIENDS, AND THE teams you root for, the place where you grow up provides you with memories that infiltrate your life, time and time again. Staten Island was a great place to grow up. It was not like anywhere else in the world. If you drew a straight line from my house to Manhattan, maybe it was 20 miles, but across those 20 miles were two different worlds.

Author Norman Maclean wrote this of the Montana of his youth: "It was a world with dew on it." I don't mean to compare Staten Island to Montana, but I know what Maclean was talking about. The neighborhoods were all *new*—the streets, the sidewalks, the schools. When we moved into our house in 1968, there were only three houses on the street; the rest were built over the next five years.

Our town was small but included, as most towns did, a pizzeria, deli, dry cleaner, bagel shop, gas station, locksmith, bank, barber shop, bakery, pharmacy, and candy store. An elevated train ran directly through the middle of the town. Children rode their bikes around the neighborhood and congregated at the local candy store and pizzeria.

When my friends and I went into town, it was usually to visit Joe's Candy Store. Joe was a heavy-set old man who owned the store. He had a large round face with full lips that always held a lit cigar. I never saw Joe without a cigar in his mouth. I wouldn't have been surprised if he slept with it in his mouth. The store was our source for magazines, posters, wiffle balls, stick-ball bats, and of course, candy.

Joe usually sat in the back room of the store, which was sectioned off by a bright green curtain. Whenever we entered the store, the bells on the door jingled, the curtain opened, and a blast of hazy cigar smoke filled the air. Then Joe came out. The back room was where Joe and his friends played cards during the day.

The best part of Joe's Candy Store was the large hot pretzels he sold. Many times we'd be playing in the park or the schoolyard and someone would say, "Hey, let's go to Joe's for pretzels!" No one ever said no. We jumped on our bikes and rode to Joe's. He would heat the pretzels on a grill in the back of the store until they were hot and crunchy. We always bought a small bottle of Coke too. I don't know why, but the Coke always tasted better in the bottle—and it still does.

After we got our pretzels and sodas, we sat outside the store and talked about football and baseball and how one day each one of us was going to play professional ball.

In our neighborhood, the children played outside for hours. There were no play dates, no grown-ups watching you, no parents hovering over your every move, no parents on the scene to "stick up" for you. If you fell off your bike, you got up, scraped off your knee, and continued to ride—no Neosporin, no Bacitracin, no first-aid cream, no peroxide... not even a Band-Aid! I mean, really, who was going to go home just to get a Band-Aid? If you were playing in the schoolyard and the older kids came along and wanted the field, you had two choices: leave or fight for the field.

Today, lots of things are very "touchy-feely" and everything needs to be discussed. Parents are *very* involved in their kids' lives. They try to make kids share all the time... and work out their differences all the time...and talk about their feelings all the time. They try to make the older kids explain why they took the field from the smaller kids in the first place. Where I grew up, and because of the way I grew up, and because of the time in which I grew up, I learned early on what the answer to that question invariably was: *because I could!*

I never knew the names of any of the stores in town. Neither did my friends or our parents. If my mom needed meat, she would say "Go see Frank the Butcher and tell him I need a pound of chopped meat." There was Frank the Butcher, Tony the Pharmacist, Pete the Barber, and Fred the Dry Cleaner, among others. We *knew* the owners and they all *knew* us. They were our neighbors. They were our friends.

Their children were our friends. We were their children's friends. It was like one big family.

It was a time when life had a consistency and an order to it. It was a time when all things seemed to mean more. Your family, your friends—they weren't just people in your life; they *were* your life. In a six block radius I had thirteen first cousins. Family wasn't just people you saw on holidays; they were people who were part of your everyday life. We had everyday relationships with them. We played together; we ate together; we were happy together; we were sad together. Friends weren't just people you saw at baseball practice or who your parents had to coordinate play dates with. They lived next door to you, across the street, or around the corner. You were always in their house or they were in yours. Your entire day consisted of what you and your friends wanted it to be. No major interference from adults. You left in the morning and had to be back for dinner.

It was a time steeped in innocence and tradition, a time when you knew who you were and where you belonged. There were some rules and many traditions... and we followed them all.

Nowhere was this more evident than on Sundays. I can't remember a Sunday that didn't seem to have an order and a purpose to it ... as well as a very specific and wonderful aroma.

# Chapter 3

## Sundays

I LAY IN MY BED AWAKE, NOT WANTING TO LEAVE THE comfort and warmth. It was early Sunday morning, and the only sound in the house came from the kitchen as my mom prepared the Sunday meal. I rolled over, looked at the bed across from me, and noticed that my brother was also awake. Neither of us said a word for a few seconds; then we smiled at each other and shouted, "Meatballs!" We jumped out of bed at the same time, ran down the hallway towards the kitchen, and stopped at the doorway waiting to be noticed. We took in the whole scene before us and inhaled the mouthwatering aroma of those meatballs.

Dad sipped his coffee while he read the sports section of the Sunday newspaper. Mom, of course, stood at the stove frying those meatballs and cooking a pot of pasta sauce—or "Sunday gravy" as some people called it. The sauce was in a large pot, much larger than anything needed for just a family of five. In the pot with the sauce were sausages, spare ribs, and "bracciole" (pronounced something like 'bra-ziol'). On the counter-top was a large dish that was already piled high with cooked meatballs waiting to be submerged in the red, bubbling, hot pool of sauce.

Mom finally turned her head away from the stove, noticed us in the doorway, and came to give us both a big hug and a kiss. "Good morning boys! Did you sleep okay? You guys hungry?"

"Yeah, yeah, yeah!" we yelled, and nodded our heads excitedly.

"Okay, I'll get you something," she said, and headed back to the stove.

I laughed to myself. Every Sunday, it was the same. *"Okay, I'll get you something,"* she'd say, and then bring each of us a dish with two huge meatballs on it. My brother and I devoured those soft, sizzling meatballs very quickly. Even now, when I wake up on a Sunday, I can smell them sometimes!

After breakfast, I showered and left the house through the garage, grabbing my bike. Within minutes my friends arrived with their own bikes. They were my closest friends: John, Tommy, Steve, Andy, and Tony. We all lived within two blocks of each other. John was my best friend. We had known each other since we were four years old. I can't explain why we were best friends. Maybe it was just because he lived right next door, with his bedroom directly across from mine and separated only by the twenty feet between our houses.

We just always seem to fit together. What I do know is that we never fought, never got tired of hanging out together, and never ever let anyone play us off each other. We were fiercely loyal to each other.

We rode our bikes, laughing and joking, until we arrived at our local church for the 10 o'clock mass. We went to the 10 o'clock mass because the other masses were too early, and because Father Valenti always "served" the 10 o'clock mass.

My friends and I had known Father Valenti since we were very little. He was a short, stocky man in his early forties but exuded the enthusiasm of someone half his age. Father Valenti had a way of making us understand the many concepts and morals from his sermons. He made it easy for us to get up to go to church on Sundays. Maybe that's why we were close to him and considered him a real friend.

As usual when the mass ended, he was there to greet us at the church doors.

"Good morning boys," he said, with a large smile. "Good to see you on this beautiful Sunday morning."

Steve moved in front of Father Valenti, shaking his hand. "Are you kidding, Father? I wouldn't miss this for anything," he said, somewhat sarcastically.

Father Valenti looked at him for a moment, and then answered, matching his tone: "Well, I did notice that you stayed awake for the *whole* mass."

Tony jumped in: "It wasn't easy."

We all laughed. Father Valenti's eyes twinkled a bit as he enjoyed the joke. "I'll remember that when I'm giving out your science and religion grades!" Everyone appreciated the humor, and then Father Valenti sent us on our way. "Have a great day boys."

We grabbed our bikes and headed into town.

Every Sunday morning after church we stopped at Fiorelli's Bakery. We could smell the fragrance of delicious, warm, Italian breads and pastries a half a block away, making our mouths water. The store was always crowded, with the line stretching outside the door. But *we* never waited on line. We walked in and were greeted by Mr. Fiorelli. Mr. Fiorelli was the owner, the baker, and Steve's father. "Good'a mornin' boys." Each of us said hello as we walked behind the counter and grabbed a cookie. "Were'a you good'a boys at'a church?" he asked.

"Yep, we stayed awake the whole time," answered Tony.

"That's a good. You learn'a anyt'ing?"

"Yeah, but it's too complicated," I said.

Mr. Fiorelli laughed heartily and turned towards the back counter, grabbed several large, brown paper bags—each bearing one of our last names—and handed them out to us. Our parents would place their Italian bread and dessert orders during the week and we would pick up the bags after church. We thanked Mr. Fiorelli and made our way towards the door. "You boys have a good'a day!" he shouted, and we waved goodbye until the next week.

After mounting our bikes, we looked at each other and smiled. Without saying a word, we each opened our bag and inhaled deeply, the aroma of that freshly baked bread filling our lungs.

This too was part of our Sunday ritual, and oh yes...I can still smell the aroma of that freshly baked bread whenever I think about it.

My friends and I said goodbye to each other and rode our bikes home to deliver the bread bags to our families. When I got home, I dropped my bike on the lawn and hurried into the house. I ran up the steps, and handed my mom the bread, barely stopping before joining my brother, David, who was (by this time) sitting in front of the TV. I looked at the clock. It was 11:30.

"Which one is it'? I asked David.

"I don't know; it hasn't come on yet."

Every Sunday morning, on Channel 11, an Abbott & Costello film was broadcast. David and I always watched it and sometimes our sister, Jackie, joined us.

Just before the conclusion of the movie, the doorbell rang. Aunt Connie's family was always the first to arrive for Sunday dinner. Never ones to arrive empty handed, Aunt Connie and her husband, Uncle Paul, and their three children entered the house with several large dishes of food. Moments later, Mom's sister, Aunt Joanne, her husband, Uncle Tom, and their five children arrived—also bringing food. Sundays were always a feast day as well as a family day!

Dad emerged from the kitchen, carrying two large, chilled glasses of beer for Uncle Paul and Uncle Tom, and then they quickly headed down to the den for the one o'clock football game. Mom and my aunts moved into the kitchen, to discuss the events of the week that had just passed and put the finishing touches on the food we would soon devour. My cousins scattered inside and outside the house until dinner time.

Sunday dinner was always served at 2:30, which (not coincidentally) was halftime of the first football game. We ate hungrily, heartily, and happily.

Uncle Rich always arrived just before the second football game began. I'm sure this had something to do with the activities of a single man on Saturday nights. After he said hello to everyone, Mom made him a big plate of food and poured him a huge drink.

He sat at the table, took a few bites of his meal, and then asked my mother, "Is it okay if I go down to the den and watch the games with the others?" Every week she said, "Of course, enjoy the game." She never said "no", but every week he asked—not because he had to, but because he loved and respected her. Seeing that as a child left an impression on me that has never faded. Never take your loved ones for granted.

In New York, the second football game on Sundays (the four o'clock game) was usually either a Jets game or a Giants game, but six or seven times a year, NBC would show a doubleheader game. Due to their national appeal and the number of star players, the Oakland Raiders were usually chosen for this doubleheader game. The Raiders were also broadcast two or three times a year on ABC's *Monday Night Football*. This was perfect for my family, because we were all huge Raiders fans and this was the only way for us to see a Raiders game. During those years, I bet we probably saw eight or nine of the Raiders' fourteen regular season games.

As the afternoon games came to a close, the entire family gradually migrated to the den. When the games ended, NBC immediately aired *Mutual of Omaha's Wild Kingdom*, followed by the *Wonderful World of Disney*. The whole family watched these shows together. Afterward, we all gathered around the table again, one last time, for dessert, before everyone headed home to start a new week.

Every Sunday night, I got into bed knowing that I was surrounded by people who loved me, and deep down I knew that would never change.

I know that, by today's standards, it might seem a little simple, but to us there was no other way. My whole world was contained in that neighborhood and populated by the family and friends who filled my life. The streets were tree lined and quiet, and at night we fell asleep under starlit black skies. Looking back on it now, it still feels safe.

It was as perfect a place and time as I've ever known, and I thought it would last forever.

# CHAPTER 4

## CHRISTMAS

I LOVE CHRISTMAS. I ALWAYS HAVE. I'VE ALSO ALWAYS loved football. So it's understandable that these two loves would be part of some of the most significant and memorable moments of my life.

Christmas was not just a one-day holiday in our house, nor was it a two-day holiday, celebrating just Christmas Eve and Christmas Day. No, in our house it was, in fact, a month-long celebration of faith, family, and food. For my family, Christmas actually began on Friday, the day after Thanksgiving, with my father heading up to the attic very early in the morning to bring down the Christmas decorations and tree. In a short time, the entire living room was covered with boxes. My brother, sister, and I opened them one at a time and "announced" every single item in the box before placing it on the Christmas tree.

"Here's the Batman ornament."

"Oh, look, it's the lights!"

"Wow, here's the ornament we got from Disney last year!"

"Oh, here's the baseball ornament we got at Cooperstown!"

After the tree was decorated and the attic cleared of all Christmas boxes, my father, with some help from my brother, David, and me, decorated the outside of the house. By Saturday evening, the entire house was decorated inside and out.

On the Sunday after Thanksgiving, all my aunts, uncles, and cousins gathered at our house—not only for Sunday dinner but also to make our family's traditional Christmas Fruit Cake, to begin planning the Christmas Eve and Christmas Day meals, and to bake Christmas cookies, which we would devour not only on Christmas Day but throughout the entire month of December. For an Italian family like mine, it wasn't enough to just bake *some* cookies. We baked about ten different kinds of cookies for Christmas: fig cookies, butter cookies, mostraccioli (cookies with a special wine and chocolate sauce), biscotti, chocolate chip cookies, almond cookies, rainbow cookies, lemon ricotta cookies, and of course, pignoli cookies (Sicilian Macaroons) ... just to name a few.

By the end of the day, our house *was* a bakery, and smelled just as good as Mr. Fiorelli's.

So the house was decorated, the cookies were baked—some were put in Christmas tins (so we could eat them), some were frozen (so they would last till Christmas)—the Christmas menus were planned out, the fruit cake was made and soaking in rum, and Christmas was still four weeks away. This was perfect for my mother and my aunts, because this meant they had plenty of time to plan and shop for the baking of the Christmas cakes and pies: carrot cake, Italian cheesecake, apple pie, pumpkin pie, and various fruit pies. Once again, our house became a bakery.

The rest of the month was devoted to talking about and preparing for the Christmas Eve and Christmas Day meals. Mom and Dad would constantly review and update the menu, and every year they would have the same argument, which centered around a particular fish dish called "baccala". My dad loved it.

"Barbara," he would start, "don't forget to put baccala on your shopping list."

Mom couldn't stand to look at it, much less cook it as part of a holiday meal, and so she would try to get out of it. "Really Anthony, I think we have enough food on the menu."

"Okay, Barbara, just make sure the baccala is on it."

I loved all kinds of seafood, and still do, but my mom was right about the baccala. Firstly, anything called "baccala" can't possibly taste good, but believe me, the smell was worse than the taste. There is only one way to describe this smell: Take an old sock, wear it on your foot for a month, take it off, put some old cheese in it, and leave it outside in the sun for a week. Can you smell it? That's what baccala smells like. Got the picture?

Despite the baccala, which is actually dry, salted codfish, our Christmas Eve meal was my favorite meal of the holidays. Also known as "The Feast of the Seven Fishes", we always began our feast with baked clams, fried calamari (squid), and pulpo (octopus) salad. This was usually followed by a main course of fried shrimp, spaghetti with sauce and crabs, mussels marinara, stuffed calamari, and of course, baccala. Mom always gave in and made it; it was Christmas, after all.

Why seven types of fish? The origin of eating only seafood on Christmas Eve commemorates the birth of baby Jesus. As a sign of respect for this Holy occurrence, animal flesh is not eaten. It also commemorates the fact that God rested from His work on the seventh day. Seven is the most repeated number in the Bible and appears over seven hundred times. Whatever the reason, it is a tradition that my family continues to this day, and it truly remains a feast.

This voluminous seven-fish dinner was usually followed by the singing of Christmas carols and the telling of stories of Christmases past, but no matter what, there was always the reminder that Christ was the focal point of the holiday.

As the night drew on, my father and uncles took over the dining-room table for games of poker. As a small child, I was always amazed by all the money on the table, but in reality they were only betting nickels, dimes, and quarters. By 11:30, some of the adults and the older children had left for Midnight Mass, while the smaller children were sent to bed, comforted by the fact that, when they awoke, Santa Claus would have arrived and left presents for all.

Today, many of these traditions that we held dear are challenged, changed, and sometimes even eliminated, but I can tell you without hesitation that it was these traditions that comforted us, kept our families together, and in many ways shaped the people we would ultimately become.

We were an average, middle-class family, but somehow my parents always made Christmas morning amazing. Although each Christmas had its own feel and its own memories, Christmas mornings always seemed the same, and it was this that made the anticipation of Christmas even more exciting.

My sister, Jackie, was always the first one up. She ran into the bedroom that my brother and I shared and shouted, "Wake up, guys! Wake up! Wake up! *Santa Claus came! He came!*" She would jump on each of our beds to make sure that we woke up immediately, barely missing jumping on top of us. "Come on, guys! Wake up! Wake up! Santa was here!" After shaking off the effects of the night's sleep—although, I really don't know how we managed to sleep at all—the three of us practically raced to our parents' bedroom to wish them a Merry Christmas, eager to get to the presents that waited for us under the tree.

Along the way, my sister—still unable to contain her excitement—would sing her own song: "*Santa Claus came, Santa Claus came. I heard him last night.*"

Turning to her, David asked, "Did he eat the cookies?"

"Yes! All of them. And he drank the milk too!"

We entered our parent's room and shouted "Merry Christmas! Merry Christmas!" as loud as we could, and jumped on their bed. My parents, startled by the sudden noise, quickly realized that it was Christmas morning.

"Okay, we're coming; we're coming," my father said, as my mother reached for the three of us. "Christmas kisses?" she would ask. "Where are my Christmas kisses?"

As we lined up and gave her a great big hug and a Christmas kiss, my dad sat at the foot of the bed trying to shake the sleepiness from his head. "Merry Christmas kids!"

"Merry Christmas Dad!" we shouted, excitedly.

"Did Santa come?" My father asked, knowing full well what the answer was.

"Yes! Yes he did! He did!" said my sister, with a great big grin on her face.

"Well, let's go see what he brought you this year."

And so we sprinted out of their bedroom and towards the living room, where all the presents awaited under the magnificent tree. Each of us looked for the presents with our names on them; each of us made a pile of our own; each of us took turns opening our presents.

"Oh, yes! I got Barbie!"

"I got a G.I. Joe!"

"I got a football!"

"Oh, yippee, I got a baseball bat!"

"Oh, I got a beautiful dress!"

"Yay! I got a 'Lite-Brite'...just what I wanted!"

The living room filled with the sound of tearing paper, and the *oohing* and *ahhing* that accompanied the excited announcement of our gifts, because they were (invariably) exactly what we had been eagerly hoping for practically all year long.

My parents always stood side by side, arms around each other, and watched the Christmas morning unfold before their eyes. It was hard to miss the look of joy and contentment on their faces as they watched our excitement.

After the presents were opened, my dad gathered the family in front of the tree, and asked us all to hold hands. Then he would gently unfold a small piece of paper and begin to read:

**"And there were in the same country shepherds abiding in the field, keeping watch over their flock by night.**

**And, lo, the angel of the Lord came upon them, and the glory of the Lord shone round about them: and they were sore afraid.**

**And the angel said unto them, Fear not: for, behold, I bring you good tidings of great joy, which shall be to all people.**

**For unto you is born this day in the city of David a Savior, which is Christ the Lord.**

**And this shall be a sign unto you; Ye shall find the babe wrapped in swaddling cloths, lying in a manger.'**

And suddenly there was with the angel a multitude of the heavenly host praising God, and saying, 'Glory to God in the highest and on earth peace, good will toward men.'"

# Chapter 5

# The Team

Besides Christmas, my other great love was football, specifically the Oakland Raiders. The Raiders were my favorite football team and the favorite football team of my entire family. My father, uncles, and cousins were all Raiders fans. I know this must seem weird—a New York family rooting for a team from Oakland—but there was a definite reason for this.

My dad and his family grew up in Brooklyn, New York. His father died suddenly in early 1945, at a young age, and his mother was left with three children to raise and care for on her own: Aunt Connie, who was ten years old at the time, my father, who was seven, and Uncle Rich, who was six. Grieving the loss of her husband, she had no choice but to go to work, which forced her to spend many hours away from her children, who were themselves grieving the loss of their father. Fortunately, she had become very good friends with her next door neighbors and they chipped in to help out with the children. The neighbors, Louis and Rose Davis, had recently moved to Brooklyn from Brockton, Massachusetts.

The youngest of their two sons was named Al. Al was a junior at Erasmus High School when my grandfather died. Every day after school he taught my dad and Uncle Rich to play football. Football came easy for Al. He was a natural athlete, but it was in the finer points of the game that Al excelled. My father listened for hours as Al diagrammed plays in the street, using rocks to represent the players in the formations. Al enjoyed teaching football, and my father, who was looking to fill the void created by the loss of his father, looked to him as an older brother who helped fill in the hours of loneliness. Al sparked a passion for football in my father that continued throughout his life.

Al Davis left Brooklyn after high school to attend college, and eventually became an assistant football coach at Adelphi College in New York. He parlayed that job into the head coaching job at Ft. Belvoir, VA., while serving in the Army. He then spent a year as a scout for the Baltimore Colts, before returning to college football as an assistant at The Citadel and then Southern California. The Los Angeles Chargers hired him to work under offensive mastermind Sid Gillman as an offensive ends coach. Occasionally, Al returned to Brooklyn and always found time to spend with my dad, telling him stories about the new American Football League.

Then Al Davis was hired as head coach and general manager of the three-year-old Oakland Raiders team. As coach, he took a team that had finished 1-13 the previous year to the second best record in the AFL, at 10-4. It was the biggest one-year turn around in pro-football history, and the Associated Press named him Coach of the Year. Eventually, he became the team's owner.

My father saw less of Al as time went on, but the combination of Al's true friendship and the success of the Raiders turned him and my entire family into lifelong Raiders fans.

Under Davis' leadership, the Raiders became one of the greatest franchises in sports history. From 1967 to 1977, they were the most successful football team in the NFL. Their record in those 11 seasons was an amazing 119-28-7. The Raiders weren't just a team, they were a gang—a gang who snubbed their noses at the NFL establishment and ushered in a new method for football success. Even their uniforms were intimidating: silver pants with solid black jerseys, topped off by a silver helmet that featured a one-eyed pirate, and swords in the background on both sides. They were known as the "Pride and Poise Boys" and slogans such as "Commitment to Excellence" and "Just Win Baby" became Raiders trademarks. The Raiders became part of American pop culture. There was even a poem dedicated to them, written by former NFL Films President and Co-founder Steve Sabol, titled "The Autumn Wind."

**The autumn wind is a pirate Blustering in from sea.**

**With a rollicking song, he sweeps along, Swaggering boisterously.**

**His face is weather beaten.**

**He wears a hooded sash, With a silver hat about his head, And a bristling black mustache.**

**He growls as he storms the country, A villain big and bold.**

**And the trees all shake and quiver and quake, As he robs them of their gold.**

**The autumn wind is a Raider, Pillaging just for fun.**

**He'll knock you 'round and upside down, And laugh when he's conquered and won.**

In the eleven-year period from 1967 to 1977, the Raiders appeared in eight American Football Conference (AFC) Championship Games, and represented the AFL in Super Bowl II, losing to the legendary Green Bay Packers 33-14. Regular season success was easy, but getting back to the Super Bowl proved to be far more elusive for the silver and black.

In the eight years following their Super Bowl appearance, the Raiders played in six AFC Championship games. They lost them all. Six chances to go to the Super Bowl and they did not win any of them.

They lost to the New York Jets in 1968.

They lost to the Kansas City Chiefs in 1969.

They lost to the Baltimore Colts in 1970.

They lost to the Miami Dolphins in 1973.

They lost to the Pittsburgh Steelers in 1974.

They lost to the Steelers again in 1975.

Six chances in eight years to go to the Super Bowl and they lost every time. If there was a silver lining in the losses it was that all six teams they lost to went on to win the Super Bowl. Whenever his team lost, Dad would say the same thing to me: "If you lose, you want to lose to the team that wins the championship. That way, at least you know you lost to the best team."

The Raiders did not make it to the AFC Championship game in 1972, but what happened in their divisional playoff game would become part of NFL legend. I was only eight years old at the time, but I remember it well...not so much the game, but the way my father and uncles reacted to history unfolding before their eyes.

The Raiders were playing the Steelers in the divisional round of the playoffs. In frozen Three Rivers Stadium, the two teams squared off in a fierce defensive struggle.

The Steelers managed two field goals and held a 6-0 lead with less than two minutes to go in the 4th quarter. On a key third down play, Raider quarterback Ken Stabler, not known for his running skills, crossed up the Steelers and took off, running uncontested to the 3-yard line, where he dove into the end zone.

Raiders-7

Steelers-6

The Steelers got the ball back with 1:21 left in the game. After three unsuccessful plays, the Steelers were faced with 4^{th} down and ten on their own 40-yard line, with only twenty-two seconds to play. What unfolded next became the most talked about play in the history of the National Football League.

Steeler quarterback Terry Bradshaw took the snap and faded back to pass. Raider lineman Tony Cline reached for Bradshaw but he spun away. Bradshaw faded to his left, away from the oncoming rush and fired a pass to Steeler running back Frenchy Fugqua. The ball and Raider defensive back Jack Tatum arrived at the same time, and the ball was knocked back to the line of scrimmage. The ball was caught just before it hit the ground by Steeler running back Franco Harris. Harris cradled the ball and ran down the sideline untouched for a touchdown and victory.

Steelers-13

Raiders-7

I watched as my father and uncles stood and yelled at the television as the announcer repeated his shock at the play. Replays were inconclusive as to whether the ball was touched by the Raiders or the Steelers prior to Harris' reception, but nevertheless, the referee once again signaled touchdown.

The play was called the Immaculate Reception and would go on to be the most famous play in NFL history. I was only eight years old, but I went to Catholic school, so I knew that if a play was called Immaculate, you didn't stand much of a chance.

Once again the Raiders were denied. Time was running out on the organization that placed winning above all else. The Raiders needed to win it all in 1976, or history would forever label them as a team that just "couldn't win the big one".

# CHAPTER 6

# WINNING THE BIG ONE

THE RAIDERS DID FINALLY WIN "THE BIG ONE". FOR THE team and their fans, the heartbreak finally disappeared in 1976. That year, the Raiders went 13-1, the best record in the NFL. Their only loss was to the New England Patriots in week four. They went on to win their last ten games, but it was the second to last game of the regular season that showed all of America exactly what the Raiders were made of.

The defending champion and Raider nemesis Pittsburgh Steelers had started the season 1-4 and looked as if their season was a lost cause. But the Steelers were a proud team and rebounded, winning their next nine games to finish at 10-4. Amazingly, the Steelers allowed only 28 points in those last nine games. 28 points in nine games! Only 3 points per game! No one in the league wanted to play the Steelers in the playoffs.

**EXCEPT THE RAIDERS!**

In week 13 of the regular season, the Raiders were scheduled to play the Cincinnati Bengals who were tied with the Steelers. The Raiders had the best record in the league and had already clinched home field advantage for the playoffs. They had nothing to play for.

**EXCEPT RAIDER PRIDE!**

A win by the Bengals, and the Steelers were out of the playoffs. A Raider win and the Steelers were in. Sportswriters throughout the country predicted a Raider dive.

"The Raiders don't want to play the Steelers."

"The Raiders will lie down."

**THE RAIDERS WOULD HAVE NONE OF IT.**

Interviewed prior to the game, Raider coach John Madden boasted, "We are afraid of no one; we will win." The Raiders did more than win. They crushed the Bengals 35-20, and squashed any doubts that they feared the Steelers. Years later, Madden would say that it was the proudest win he ever had.

Chants of "We *want* the Steelers" were heard throughout the "Raider Nation", and the Raiders *got* the Steelers. After a scare in the first round, the Raiders snuck past the New England Patriots 24-21, and for the third year in a row, the Steelers stood between the Raiders and the Super Bowl, which had eluded them for so long. The Raiders had arrived at this point only to be turned away too many times.

The time had come for this Raider team to finally rid itself of this failure. The Raiders played an almost flawless game and defeated the hated Steelers 24-7. They were AFC Champions for the first time since 1967 and would play in Super Bowl XI.

The Raiders arrived at the Super Bowl ready to claim the greatness they always thought belonged to them. Their opponent, the Minnesota Vikings, was another team that couldn't seem to win "the big one". They'd played in three previous Super Bowls, and lost all three.

But after nine years of heartache, this Raider team would not be denied. Prior to the game, Len Dawson, the Kansas City Chiefs Hall of Fame Quarterback, offered his prediction: "The Raiders will kill 'em."

The Raider offense dominated the Vikings' famed "Purple People Eater" defense by rushing for more yards than any team in Super Bowl history. Ken Stabler skillfully picked apart the Viking secondary. Wide receiver Fred Biletnikoff grabbed four key receptions and was named Most Valuable Player.

The game was not a contest but more a coronation of Raider greatness. A decade of Raider domination culminated in the Raiders 32-14 victory in Super Bowl XI.

The wait was over. After coming so close for so many years, the Raiders had finally won "the big one".

I watched the game with my father, brother, and several uncles and cousins that day. For us, that victory was the same as winning the big prize in the lottery. I watched as Dad and Uncle Rich celebrated and embraced at the end.

It was a long and emotional embrace as if a great pain had been put to rest.

It was the first time that a team I rooted for had actually won a championship. Since then, I've seen "my" teams win many championships, but there's nothing like the first time—especially if you're a kid when it happens. Even now, as an adult, I can remember every detail as if it was yesterday, and know that sharing that moment with my family only made it more special.

# CHAPTER 7

# A GIRL

THROUGH THE YEARS, MY NEIGHBORHOOD CONTINUED
to grow. Foundations were poured, walls framed, and
roofs attached. One summer, the Sedona family moved
into the house directly across the street from mine and my
life changed.

On a hot, sweltering July afternoon, I sat on the curb in
front of my house and slowly bounced a pink Spalding ball
as I watched the moving men unload the large truck that was
parked in their driveway. At one point I noticed a bicycle, a
basketball, and several other toys lying on the lawn.

"*Great!*" I thought, suddenly eager and excited. "*This probably means they have kids. I hope one of them is my age!*"

A short while later, a shiny black car pulled up next to the
moving truck and a man and a woman got out. Then a girl
got out and I couldn't help staring at her. Suddenly, our eyes
met. A powerful shock and a shiver ran down my spine. I
had never felt anything like that before.

I was seven years old and I was mesmerized. I had never seen anything so beautiful. She looked like an angel. Her skin was pure and creamy white. She had velvety brown eyes the color of melted chocolate. Her brown hair was long and very shiny. I continued to stare and did not even notice that she'd walked over to me.

"Hello," she said.

I stood open mouthed, unable to stop staring at her and seemingly unable to speak.

"Hi, I'm Lauren," she offered again.

"Hi! I'm Michael" I finally answered, still unable to stop staring.

For a moment neither of us said anything. Unsure of what to do, I nervously began to bounce the ball again. Suddenly, she leaned forward and grabbed it. She held the ball out and motioned for me to back up. "Wanna play catch?"

"Sure," I said, as I moved away from her. My heart pounded in my chest and I hoped that she couldn't hear it.

We began to toss the ball back and forth to one another in silence. "So, where did you move from?" I finally asked her.

"We moved from Queens."

After our game of catch, we sat together on the curb and continued talking. "How come you moved here?"

"My dad is a fireman and he transferred to the firehouse up the street."

"Oh ... Well I hope you like it here," I said shyly, my heart still thumping loudly. We talked about our favorite colors;

we talked about our favorite sports; we talked about how many brothers and sisters we had; we talked about our favorite subjects at school; we talked about our friends; we talked about what we liked and what we didn't like. As I listened to her, I felt I had known her my entire life. We immediately became friends.

It seemed that I always felt comfortable with her; I never ran out of things to say, and I always wanted to see her. I could talk to her about anything and never felt embarrassed. She was as beautiful as a princess, as caring as my mother, and yet she could throw a baseball like any of my friends.

Although most of our free time was spent with our own friends, we somehow always managed to find each other. Often, we would both get home at the same time and would meet in the middle of our street to touch base with each other. Neither of us wanted to be the first to say goodbye. As we got older, we would just walk around the neighborhood for a while. The walks were a way for us to stay close to each other while we were growing up in separate directions.

It was one of those walks, on a spring evening in 1976 that ultimately led to a discovery that would deepen our friendship even further.

# Chapter 8

# The Roof

It was a clear and crisp spring evening and the sun was beginning to set. I walked home alone, football in hand. When I turned the corner, I noticed Lauren walking towards me. She saw me and waved. We met in the middle of the street and I tossed the ball to her.

"Hey"

"What's going on?" she asked

"Same old stuff."

"Yeah, I know," she said, tossing the football back.

"Wanna walk?" I asked, hoping she would join me.

"Sure," she replied, trying not to show her excitement.

We walked side by side, tossing the football back and forth to each other. The conversation moved from school, to friends, to music. We ended up near the local grammar school and she motioned for me to go out for a long pass. "Hey! Biletnikoff! Go deep!"

I ran away from her, looking for the pass. She leaned back and threw the ball with all her might. It sailed right over my head, over the school fence, and landed behind a tree.

I turned to her. "Nice throw," I said, sarcastically.

"I'm sorry." She raised her shoulders and buried her head in her hands, trying to contain her laughter.

The fence was about six feet high and in a section of the school that was not normally accessible to students. I climbed the fence, searched for the ball, and disappeared behind a group of trees. Then I called out to her. "Hey, check this out!"

"What?"

"Come over the fence," I answered.

"I'm not climbing the fence!"

"I'm serious! Come on over here."

With a sigh of resignation, she climbed over the fence and moved towards me as I waited behind the trees. "Well, here I am," she whispered. "What is it?"

I pointed to a steel ladder that was attached to the school building. With our eyes, we followed the ladder upward and saw that it continued up to the third floor.

"Let's go up!" I said excitedly.

"Yes! C'mon"

We climbed the ladder to the third floor and walked across it, only to discover another ladder, which went up two more floors to the roof. "Well, now we have to go all the way up," challenged Lauren. I nodded, quickly taking her up on the challenge, and began to climb the ladder again, this time all the way to the top.

The view left us both speechless. The breathtaking display of the setting sun and the evening lights created a spectacular vision of our entire town. It was as if we were seeing its beauty for the first time.

Looking around, I noticed a bench and motioned for Lauren to follow me there. "This is just so cool!" I said, as we sat down next to each other.

"Very cool" she agreed. We sat in silence for a while and continued to gaze at the amazing view before us.

I turned to face her, and whispered, "We can't tell anybody about this."

She agreed immediately and shook her head. "No way, this is our secret."

We watched in silence as darkness continued to fall over our town and made the scene before us even more magnificent.

The roof became our special place. A place where no one could find us, no one could hear us, and no one could bother us—a place where we could be alone together. When one of us was upset, we went to the roof to talk. When we hadn't seen each other for a while, we went to the roof to talk. Sometimes we went to the roof just to admire the view. It was our way of reconnecting as our lives sometimes moved us in different directions.

One early spring night, as the sun was setting, we climbed up to our special place, sat on our bench, and admired the view. I started to tell her about my day but realized that she really wasn't listening. She had a pensive look on her face, and before I had a chance to finish my story, she asked, "What to do want to be when you grow up?"

Surprised by her question, I stood up. "What?"

"What do want to be when you grow up?" she repeated. "Come on, you gotta have some idea."

I paused for a moment, sat down again, and started to think about it, but I already knew what my answer was. Deep down inside me, I had known the answer for quite a while. "I want to be a wide receiver for the Oakland Raiders."

She wasn't surprised at all. "Like Biletnikoff?"

"Yeah, just like him."

"Why him?"

I leaned in closer to her and whispered reverently, "Have you ever seen him play?"

"No."

"Oh, you've got to see Freddy! He's not the biggest guy, not the fastest guy, but he's smart! Smarter than the other guys ..." I rambled on as I stood up again, unable to contain my excitement or my emotions, "... and his hands...anything that touches his hands is a catch. Sometimes I think, if he made it, why can't I? I'm fast and I've got good hands." I paused, and then quietly said, "I don't know ... it's just something I think about." I looked away for a moment, barely daring to imagine my dream as reality.

Taken aback by my emotion, Lauren was silent for a few seconds, and then asked "Football players make a lot of money, right?"

I sat down next to her again. "No, it's not that."

She touched my arm, and then whispered, "What is it?"

I tried again to explain but just couldn't find my voice.

She smiled at me gently. "What is it?"

I looked down at the ground and began talking, my voice quiet and almost cracking with emotion. "My father ... he loves the Raiders. I can't imagine how he would feel if I ever played for them. If I pulled that black jersey over my head, put that silver helmet on, and ran out onto the field with the sun shining...I just don't think I could ever give him anything better."

I had just shared something that was so special to me, something I wouldn't share with just anyone. Lauren gave me a bright smile and I knew that she understood. She knew it was my special dream. I regained my composure and turned to her. "What about you?"

"What?" The smile slowly left her face.

"What do *you* want to be?"

"No."

"Oh, come on...I told *you.*"

She hesitated, and then said (not particularly convincingly), "I'd like to be a music teacher."

I realized that she was hiding something, so I persisted. "Come on, there's something else." She still didn't answer. "Come on."

"No, it's stupid."

"It's not stupid," I said. "Come on, tell me."

She answered very quickly, as if to dismiss what she was going to say. "I just want to get married and have kids."

I couldn't help myself and started laughing. "*What?*"

"See, I knew you would think ..."

Seeing the hurt in her eyes, I quickly realized my insensitivity and rushed in, "No, no, no! I'm sorry. I'm really sorry! Go ahead. I'm really gonna listen."

She started cautiously. "Well, I never had any brothers or sisters. I never had someone to play with on rainy days when I couldn't go out. I never had a little brother or sister to ask me for advice...never had a brother who wanted to play catch or a sister who wanted me to braid her hair or paint her nails. I never had a brother or sister to take care of or who could take care of me. I just think that of all the jobs I could eventually have, well ... what could be better than that? I would love to do all those things with my own kids. I know this is silly. All my friends want to be doctors and lawyers or important stuff like that."

I was taken aback and yet impressed by what she had said. "It's not silly," I said, with complete sincerity. "It's not silly at all. My mom's not a doctor or lawyer and I think she's great.

I bet someday your kids will think that you're great too. And you know what? They'd be right."

Lauren smiled, gave me a big hug, and whispered in my ear, "Thank you."

Together, we quietly watched the sunset as we sat side by side, on our bench ... on our rooftop.

I loved being Lauren's friend. Our friendship continued to grow and the rooftop became the place where we would share many special moments.

We both kept the secret.

# Chapter 9

# July 4, 1976

On July 4, 1976, I awoke to a clear, beautiful summer's day. It was a special day—the two hundredth birthday of the United States of America. On my way to the kitchen for breakfast, I stopped at the television to watch the news. The Statue of Liberty and New York City Harbor were surrounded by boats from all over the world, come to celebrate the day. It was a spectacular sight. There was a copy of the *Daily News* on our living room table with "HAPPY BIRTHDAY AMERICA!" sprawled in large print across the front page.

I wanted to spend some time with my friends before my relatives came over to celebrate the day with us, and so after breakfast I headed out the door to meet them.

When I stepped outside, the scene before me caught me by surprise and for a brief moment I thought that this was not the street where I lived. Somehow, it had been transformed into a red, white, and blue tribute to America. Giant

American flags hung from flag poles on every house and red, white, and blue adorned all front windows. The street lamps and fire hydrants were decked out with red, white, and blue ribbons and "Happy Birthday America" signs dangled from many tree branches. In front of all the houses there were tables draped with red, white, and blue tablecloths, and many families had rolled their barbeques to the front of their houses. My parents and our neighbors (the adults of course) had worked throughout the night to create this magical scene of red, white, and blue.

As I stood outside, admiring the view and listening to the sound of fireworks in the distance, my father walked up beside me. Dad looked around and declared, "Greatest country in the world." I looked up at him curiously. "You know why?' he asked.

"No, not really" I replied, shaking my head.

He smiled affectionately at me, and put his hand on my shoulder. "Because here in America you can be anything you want to be. America is hope...not just for us, but for people all over the world." Dad looked up at the clear blue sky and continued. "When you have hope, you are a rich man... because with hope, all things are possible."

I took a moment to reflect on this, and then eagerly asked him, "You mean I can be anything I want to be, right?"

Dad had a way of making me understand what he was really saying. I think he said these types of things because he wanted us to always aspire to our dreams, to never give up—no matter how many times we got knocked down—and to always remember how lucky we were to be living in a country that allowed us to do all this.

I helped him bring our BBQ to the front of the house and then happily took off to meet my friends at the top of the street.

They were huddled in a circle. John held a Ken doll that he had taken from his sister's room. "Okay, let's put a fire-cracker in his shirt pocket," he said, the excitement quite clear in his voice.

"Put one in the pocket of his pants," Andy added.

I suddenly realized that Steve was there, but not actually in the circle of friends. He stood off to the side, quietly watching and listening to us while he sipped a large Cherry Slurpee. "What about his butt?" he asked shamelessly.

Startled by what he had just blurted out, we all turned to look at him in disbelief. Unwilling to pass on the chance to make fun of him, Tony quickly responded. "You know … there really is something seriously wrong with you!" Then he made the crazy sign with his index finger, swirling it around the side of his head. We all laughed; the humor of the situation not lost on us boys.

"*What?!*" Steve glared, not only at Tony but also at us. "Well, *I* think it would be really funny."

Tommy looked at Steve, and chuckled. "You're an idiot!"

Soon we had the doll loaded with fireworks. Then we put a play gun in its hand, posed it in a battle stance, and placed it on top of a dirt hill. We admired our handiwork for a moment, glanced at each other, and nodded. It was time to light those firecrackers. With pieces of burning rope, we lit the firecrackers simultaneously and began to run away. Steve tripped and fell, but luckily turned his head away just as the firecrackers exploded.

"All right!" I shouted.

"That was cool" Tommy added.

Steve was still on the ground about ten feet away from where we were standing, and about three feet away from where the doll was. He looked down, saw his leg covered in red, and began to scream, "Oh my God! Oh My God! My leg! My leg!" We ran over to him, and knelt down.

John immediately took control of the situation. "Calm down! Calm down! Where is it? Where's the cut?"

Steve continued screaming, "I don't know! It hurts!"

Andy looked up and down Steve's leg. "I don't see a cut. I don't even see a burn."

Tommy then noticed Steve's cup lying on the ground. He looked at Steve and then looked at the cup several times ... and then he realized what had happened. He reached down, picked up the cup, and slowly walked over to Steve.

"Hey idiot," he said, as he waved the cup in front of Steve's face. It took the rest of us a few seconds to understand what Tommy already knew.

Andy stood up, and looked Steve square in the face. "You're a moron!"

Relieved but also annoyed, John snapped, "I almost had a heart attack."

"Unbelievable." Tony added.

Steve looked closely at his leg and realized that he was fine. He then saw the empty cup that Tommy had left on the ground and became even more upset, realizing that his Slurpee was gone. We walked away, glad that our friend was okay but still a little annoyed at his mistake.

And so the day passed into night. Children ran through the street playing games and grabbing food from neighbors' tables. Music filled the air. Colorful fireworks could be seen in the night sky. Lauren's dad, Mr. Sedona—a NYC fireman— started a small fire in a handmade pit in front of his house so that everyone could toast marshmallows.

There was a sense of anticipation in the air. It was 8:50 p.m. Every year at 9:00 p.m., John's dad, Mr. DeSalle, put on the largest fireworks display in the neighborhood. I was standing with my friends, waiting for the show to start, when Lauren approached me from behind and whispered in my ear. "Can I see you a second?"

We walked away from the group.

"What's up?" I asked.

"I got an idea," she said. "You want to see?"

"Sure."

She grabbed my hand, purposely guiding me off the back end of the street so that no one could see us. When we turned the corner, she let go of my hand and started running down the street. She caught me by surprise but I quickly caught up to her.

"Where are we going?"

"You'll see," she said.

We ran a little longer, and then she stopped in front of the school.

"Come on."

She climbed over the fence and I quickly joined her. She started up to the roof and I followed her. The view at the top was breathtaking. The entire sky was covered with exploding fireworks. We could see for miles. The view was spectacular and it belonged only to us. We looked at each other.

"You're a genius," I said.

"Thank you very much," she said, as she gladly accepted her kudos and curtsied.

Lauren and I sat and watched the black sky explode in color all around us. We leaned towards each other, our arms and shoulders touching. It felt good to feel her body next to mine. Neither of us dared to move away. We watched the fireworks for the rest of the night…just the two of us.

We had left everyone else behind and didn't even notice.

# Chapter 10

# A Band

In 1972, four young men from New York set out to create a band like no band before them...a band like no other.

"We want to be the Beatles on steroids," said the band's tongue-wagging bassist.

"We don't want to be just a band," said the band's front man and lead vocalist. "We want to rule the world."

Gene Klein, Stanley Eisen, Paul Frehley, and Peter Crisscoula changed their names and became Gene Simmons, Paul Stanley, Ace Frehley, and Peter Criss. Collectively, the world would come to know them as KISS.

Acceptance within the music industry did not come fast. Music executives were put off by the band's aggressive nature, and more importantly, the make-up that covered their faces. KISS did not rule the world immediately. Their first three albums, '*KISS*', '*Hotter than Hell*', and '*Dressed to Kill*' sold modestly, but they were loud and confident, and the real essence of the band was seen during their live concerts.

Eventually, word began to spread throughout the country about this outrageous band, whose live concert just had to be seen. KISS looked great on stage, and more importantly, their songs, which lacked power on studio recordings, sounded like rock 'n roll anthems during live performances. In 1975, the band released *'KISS ALIVE'*—a double live album recorded from two concerts at COBO Hall in Detroit and consisting of sixteen songs from the first three albums.

*'KISS ALIVE',* fronted by the single, *'Rock and Roll all Night',* quickly shot up the charts, peaking at number seven on the Billboard rankings. Teenagers across America quickly became fascinated by the band's unique appearance and powerful, catchy guitar riffs.

On a September afternoon in 1975, Andy, Steve, and I were hanging out in my bedroom when John hurtled through the door holding out the *'KISS ALIVE'* album for us to see.

"Guys you gotta see this album! These guys are awesome!"

We were immediately drawn to the front cover, which showed the band in live concert poses. The cover fascinated all of us, as we had never seen such a visual band before. The power and energy of the band seemed to leap out at us.

"This is real cool!" Andy said, not actually knowing *why* it was cool.

"Let me see that!" I was curious to see what the 'awesome' was all about. John passed the album to me and I quickly opened it up. Printed on the inside cover were four handwritten letters, one from each of the band members. Fascinated,

- the four of us carefully read the letters, inexplicably feeling that these were written just for us.

The four of us were completely mesmerized by every aspect of the album and continued to pore over it. "This guy Ace looks awesome!" I said excitedly.

"Whoa, look at that demon guy!" added Andy.

"I like the drummer's make-up, and look how cool the drums are!" John put in.

While we looked at the drums, John suddenly exclaimed, "Oh man, I forgot! Look inside the album sleeve!" I looked inside and pulled out an eight-page, color booklet with photos of each band member and several group shots.

Silence engulfed the room, and four young boys who had never even heard a KISS song became instant fans.

This same scene was being played out by teenagers across America. This was the power of KISS. This is how you create a following. This is how you rule the world.

My friends and I became huge KISS fans, and as their popularity continued to rise, so did our fascination with the band. From 1976 through 1977, four more albums were released: 'Destroyer,' 'Rock-n-Roll Over,' 'Love Gun' and 'Alive II' . The make-up, costumes, and stage sets became more elaborate and the legend continued to grow. KISS had now become a world-wide phenomenon.

In the summer of 1977, KISS kicked off the *Love Gun Tour*, which included a three-night stint at New York's famed Madison Square Garden, on December 14th, 15th, and 16th.

Tickets for these concerts were a hot commodity and getting them was not an easy task.

Uncle Rich was always able to get tickets to popular events through work, so of course, I asked if he could get me some for this concert.

A few weeks after I put in my request, I was sitting in my family room reading when the phone rang, and I answered it. "Hello!"

"Hey, it's Uncle Rich. Do you have a preference which night you go?"

"What?"

"Do you want to go the first night, the last night ... which night?"

And then the light went on above my head.

"The concert? You got tickets to the concert? Really? What night? When? How? When? Really?"

At the other end of the phone, Uncle Rich laughed. "Hey Michael, are you done? Now, calm down and listen to me. I want you to sit down and just say 'yes' or 'no.'"

"Okay." I somehow managed to sit down.

"Do you want to go opening night?"

"Yes."

"Do all your friends want to go?"

"Yes."

"And their parents said it was okay?"

"Yes."

"So how many tickets should I get?"

I counted on my fingers as I shouted into the telephone, "Me, John, Andy, Tommy, Steve, Tony!...Six!"

"Okay, six," he repeated.

"No wait! My dad! My dad is taking us."

"Seven then," he confirmed. "I'll call you back in a little while."

"Does this mean we have the tickets?"

"Yes, I'll have the tickets this afternoon."

Way beyond excited, I dropped the telephone and began to run out of the house so I could tell my friends the amazing news. When I got to the front door, I realized that I had not hung up the telephone and that Uncle Rich was still waiting on the other end. I ran back to the telephone. "I'm sorry Uncle Rich, and thanks a lot! You're the best."

"All right kid, I'll see you soon."

And so my friends and I waited for the big night, while life moved on.

# Chapter 11

# August 1977

Every so often, Uncle Rich would take me fishing at Toms River in New Jersey. One very early August morning, my uncle loaded his car with my fishing gear. Yawning, I left my house, holding my tackle box, and grumbled, "Stupid fish, why don't they just eat in the afternoon like everyone else?" The fishing was always fun, but leaving the house at 4:30 in the morning just wasn't.

On the ride to Toms River, we discussed the recent events in the news: Son of Sam; the recent blackout in New York, and the looting that followed it; the Yankees; the Red Sox; and so on. Before I knew it, we were on the boat. I loved the river at that time of the morning. Stillness surrounded us. The only sound was the chirping of the birds in the trees that lined the river. Uncle Rich and I kept quiet, so as not to scare off the fish, and were rewarded for our silence. We caught about two dozen fish fairly quickly.

A few hours later, with the sun shining brightly on the river, Uncle Rich put down his fishing pole and turned towards me. "So, only two more weeks of summer vacation left. Then you start eighth grade...and then only one more year until high school."

"Yeah," I said, a little too quickly.

"What's the matter?"

"Nothing" I offered nonchalantly, hoping to change the subject.

He leaned in closer to me and quietly asked, "Hey, what's the matter?"

I really didn't want to talk about it, but I knew that his intentions were good and that I was not going to get out of answering this question. After all, we were on a boat in the middle of a river. "I don't know," I answered reluctantly. "I mean, I'm excited, ya know? It's just that I know everything will change. John and I want to go to Moore Catholic High School. Tommy and Andy want to go to Farrell High School, and Steve and Tony are definitely going to Tottenville High. We've all been together since the third grade. I feel like it's always been the six of us. I'm just afraid that it won't be that way anymore."

Uncle Rich smiled gently and an understanding look crossed his face. "Well," he began, "you're right; it won't be like it is now. It can't be. Life changes constantly. People come in and out of your life all the time. If you're lucky, you'll remember some of them. If you're really lucky, some of them will be your friends when you get older. And that's good. But what's really important is that you've all left each other with a lifetime of memories. Trust me, when you're grown up, maybe married with a couple of kids, every so often something will happen that will take you right back to this time in your life. You'll think about John, and Andy, and Tony, and all the guys. You'll think back and you'll remember. You'll remember what life felt like, what it smelled like even. You'll think back in times of happiness and smile, and in times of sadness or when life feels cold, those memories will keep you warm."

He stopped talking and gave me a pat on the back, but I sensed that he wanted to say more. After a moment, he continued. "When I was six years old," he started, looking out towards the water. "Your grandfather told me something I've never told anyone. Not even your father. We had just moved to a new neighborhood and I didn't have any new friends yet. I was sad and didn't want to go to school. One morning, I said goodbye to Mom and Dad and started to leave for school. By the time I reached our front door, tears sprang from my eyes and streamed down my face. My dad was at my side in no time, and wanted to know why I was crying. I told him that I didn't want to go to school."

"Then he hugged me and said that he understood how I felt, but that I still had to go to school.

He knelt down, looked me in the eye, and whispered softly "*Oggi se ne andra`, domani arrivera`, il sol risplendera`,* *e tutto ben sara`.*" In English, it means, 'Today will end; tomorrow will come; the sun will shine, and everything will be okay.'

"For some reason those words calmed me down and I stopped crying. Dad told me to remember that saying, and that whenever I felt upset, or scared, or sad ... I should say it to myself so that I would have the courage to go on. Those words became a secret between us."

Uncle Rich had just spoken of something that he had kept to himself for almost thirty-two years. He turned to face me, and unable to contain his emotions, his eyes filled with tears. "He died three weeks later. It's my last memory of him, and until just now, I have never repeated that saying to anyone. How about we keep this special saying a secret between you and me, just like my dad and I did?  I want you to always remember it, because you never know when you might need it."

I've never told anyone what Uncle Rich said that day. Not even my dad. It was our secret.

# Chapter 12

# September 1977

Being eighth graders afforded us the status of "kings of the school". The teachers weren't as strict as usual, and every week there seemed to be some kind of occasion that celebrated the fact that next year we would go on to high school. And so the start of the school year was fairly uneventful.

Except for Lauren.

Soon after the new school year started, things started to get weird between Lauren and me. For the first time since I knew her, I felt uncomfortable around her and found it difficult to talk to her. This was very different than when we were younger. I was always comfortable around her and always knew what to say. Now it seemed like her presence made me uncomfortable and I never knew what to say. And I didn't know why. So I started avoiding her. She must have been avoiding me too, because I suddenly realized that weeks had passed and we hadn't really seen each other outside of school.

I didn't like it.

One rainy school day, I walked into the cafeteria late for lunch. My friend Christine walked over to me.

"Hi Michael," she said, longingly. Then she entwined her arm in mine and walked with me to the food line. Christine was a pretty blonde girl I had known since grade school. I knew that she'd had a crush on me for a long time. "Where have you been? Are you going to Jim's and Jenna's party on Saturday night? I can't wait; it's gonna be lots of fun!!" She said all this in one breath and kept on going.

I barely paid attention as she rambled on about the party. I grabbed lunch and said goodbye, then headed for the table where my friends were seated, seeing Lauren on the way.

"Hello," I said, quietly. She looked at me for an instant, huffed, and deliberately turned away.

"Wow! That was really weird" I said to myself, taken aback. "What was that all about?" I knew I found it difficult to talk to her lately, but her reaction was so strong and unusual that I was really confused and a bit hurt.

During lunch, I kept glancing back at her. I guess I hoped to make eye contact with her, but she avoided looking in my direction the entire time.

Lauren walked into Religion class with Frank Binetti, both of them laughing loudly. They sat together the entire class and spoke to each other very quietly, as though they were discussing something secret. I watched them together the whole class period...and did not like it at all. It burned me inside to see her with someone else. Each time she laughed it felt like I was being punched in the stomach.

Maybe I couldn't talk to her like I used to, but I didn't want her talking to anyone else.

I didn't know what to do.

So I did nothing.

# CHAPTER 13

# NOVEMBER 1977
# FOOTBALL AGAIN ...

IN 1967, A GROUP OF MIDDLE-SCHOOL KIDS STARTED AN annual football tournament that began the first Saturday in December. The tournament included eight Catholic schools across six towns in Staten Island, and only the eighth-grade football team from each school competed. Now, the schools didn't actually have their own football teams, but every group of kids from the schools had their own neighborhood team. So these neighborhood teams "became" the school football teams.

Each year a meeting was held to kick-off the tournament, and to go over the specific rules. The meeting was always initiated by last year's winning team.

The meeting was attended by two captains from the eighth-grade teams and two captains from the seventh-grade teams. The seventh graders were included so that they would know what to do the following year. If a team did not attend the opening meeting, that team was out of the tournament for the year.

This year's meeting was initiated by the St. Charles team.

The captain of the St. Charles team was Bobby Ross. Bobby's dad was a great athlete in his day, and now Bobby was one of the best athletes in Staten Island. You name the sport—basketball, baseball, football—he was the best. For years, whenever our teams played each other, my team always lost, regardless of what sport it was.

A lot of the guys my age didn't like Bobby. They liked to say that he was arrogant or that he really wasn't that good. I think they said those things because they were jealous; he was *so* good at *everything*. I got to know him one summer when we both went to the same baseball camp, and he seemed like a good guy. I didn't think he was actually arrogant. He was just really confident, and I felt that we had a mutual respect for each other. Respect not friendship. Although I respected him, it didn't diminish my desire to beat him in the tournament.

On a gray, drizzly Saturday morning, just two days after Thanksgiving, John and I, along with the two captains from our seventh-grade team, made our way to the local Burger King. When we entered, I noticed that most of the eighth-grade football players were already seated at the tables, in teams. Two unoccupied chairs waited for John and me, and the seventh grade captains stood. We exchanged greetings with everyone and then sat down as Bobby Ross stood up and brought the annual football-tournament meeting to order.

"Okay, okay. Thanks everyone for coming. As last year's champions, St. Charles officially kicks off the 1977 tournament." Loud cheers and applause filled the room as he handed two pieces of paper and a pencil to each of the team captains.

The first piece of paper had the schedule of games printed on it as well as blank lines. This was done so the seeding of the teams could be written down by the team captains.

The second piece of paper stated the rules of the tournament in detail. These included rules such as the team captains had be present at all games, the game consisted of two thirty-minute halves, each team could only have a maximum of fifteen players, and that each team had to pick a color for the team jersey by the end of the day. The rules also specified that each team had to supply a timekeeper and that only the players and scorekeepers were allowed at the game. The most important rule was the one dictating that parents, adults or any other individuals were not allowed at the games. In fact, parents weren't even supposed to know about the games! If any of these people were noticed there, the "offending" team had to forfeit and be disqualified from the remainder of the tournament.

"Okay guys, the rules are easy to understand. Are there any questions?" Bobby asked as he looked around the room.

No one had any questions. "Good, let's go on." He motioned to his assistant captain, who stood up with a woolen ski cap in his hand. "In the cap are the names of the eight teams. The first team picked will be Team #1; the second will be Team #2, and so on. This is so we know who plays who."

Bobby reached into the hat, pulled out a piece of paper, unfolded it, and read out loud: "St. Patrick". All the captains wrote "St. Patrick" on the first blank line of their paper. Bobby continued to pull team names out of the ski cap and read them out loud. The captains wrote them all down.

When he finished, all the blank lines were filled in, and read:

1977 Tournament

1976 Champion- St. Charles

Teams:

1. St. Patrick

2. St. Thomas

3. St. Charles

4. OLSS-Our Lady Star of the Sea

5. OLQP-Our Lady Queen of Peace

6. St. Teresa

7. Holy Child

8. St. Clare

Team 1 will play Team 2 on December 3$^{rd}$ at 10:00am.

Team 3 will play Team 4 on December 3$^{rd}$ at 12:00pm.

The two winners will play on December 10$^{th}$ at 12:00pm for the right to play in the championship game.

Team 5 will play Team 6 on December 3$^{rd}$ at 2:00pm.

Team 7 will play Team 8 on December 3$^{rd}$ at 4:00pm.

The two winners will play on December 10$^{th}$ at 2:00pm for the right to play in the championship game.

The championship game will be held on December 17$^{th}$ at 2:00pm.

With nothing else to add, Bobby said, "Well, that's it guys; see you all at the first game." Then he walked away. John and I spoke to some friends from the other teams.

On our way out, a voice called out, "Hey! Parisi!" We both stopped and turned around.

"We *will* be waiting for you at the championship!" Bobby dared. "Don't let me down."

"Don't worry; we'll be there," I answered without hesitation.

As we walked out the door, John whispered, "Good move. Arrogance. I like it."

"Shut up."

# CHAPTER 14

# NOVEMBER 30, 1977

I LOVE CHRISTMAS. I ALWAYS HAVE. AND I'VE ALWAYS loved everything that has to do with Christmas. But you know that already ...

There are always many special things about Christmas time. When I was growing up, one of those special things was the Christmas shows that were shown on television. Families would gather around the television to watch shows like *Frosty the Snowman, How the Grinch Stole Christmas,* and my favorite, *Rudolph the Red-Nosed Reindeer.* There was no such thing as a VCR, or a DVD player, or an iPod, or YouTube, and these shows were only shown once a year, so you did whatever you had to do to make sure that you didn't miss them.

It was a chilly late November night. Mom and Dad were in the kitchen making popcorn the old fashioned way, because microwave popcorn didn't exist yet. My brother, sister, and I were in the living room gathered around the television...

eagerly waiting. I closed my eyes for a moment and "saw" Dad shaking the pot gently but quickly so that the popcorn wouldn't burn. We finally heard the corn start to pop and its aroma wafted into the living room.

"Yummm! Smells soooooo good!!" David said, with a great big smile on his face.

"Yeah, it does," I answered, my mouth watering.

My parents came in with five individual bowls of popcorn just as the show started. The CBS logo flashed on the screen, followed by the words: "We interrupt our regularly scheduled broadcast to bring you the following CBS Christmas Special: *Rudolph the Red-Nosed Reindeer.*"

We sat glued to the television screen and munched away at our hot popcorn, each of us reacting to the show with laughter, sadness, and ultimately, happiness as all ended well for Rudolph. Every now and then during the show, I caught my parents looking at each other. I know now that it was to acknowledge an understanding of how wonderful it was to watch their children in their youthful innocence.

When the show ended, David and Jackie clapped wildly and bounced up and down on the sofa. "Oh! Wasn't that a great show?" Mom asked, and turned to us.

"Yeah! That was great mommy!" Jackie answered, excitedly. "I wanna see it again!"

"I *loved* it!" David said.

I didn't say anything, got up from the sofa, and tried not to show that I had really enjoyed it too.

"Hey Michael, did you enjoy it?" my father called out to me, knowing that I didn't want to admit it.

"Yeah, it was good," I answered, trying not to sound interested, and left the room quickly.

I'm sure Mom and Dad smiled at each other, because they knew I really *did* like the show but thought I was too old and too cool to show it.

"Okay! It's time for bed now," said Mom, turning to David and Jackie. "Wash up, brush your teeth, then come down and say goodnight."

My brother and sister ran upstairs to get ready for bed, and I walked back into the living room. I sat down to watch the next Christmas show, *The Bing Crosby Christmas Special,* with my parents.

This was Crosby's last Christmas show, taped in London five weeks before his death. Crosby sang several songs including: "Peace on Earth" and "Little Drummer Boy" with David Bowie. Both songs later became Christmas staples.

Halfway through the show, David and Jackie came downstairs and back into the living room.

David headed for my mother. "Good night Mom."

"Good night David."

Jackie walked over to her. "Good night Mommy."

"Good night baby."

I watched as they both walked over to my father. He grabbed them and pulled them into his arms, gave them each a kiss, and whispered goodnight. Then he gave each of them a tight hug before he let them go.

"Don't forget to say your prayers," he reminded them, as they made their way to the stairs.

Jackie stopped and slowly made her way back to the living room. David followed her, curious to see what she was doing. She walked right up to my dad and asked, "Why do we pray, Daddy?" Mom, David, and I stopped and turned to face him. We all definitely wanted to hear what he had to say.

Dad seemed somewhat surprised by Jackie's question. He looked around the room at everyone, and then smiled at her. "Well, you know that God is our Father—everyone's Father. And that he gives us a lot of good things." Everyone nodded their heads in agreement. "One of the reasons we pray is to thank God for all those things. But most of the time, we pray to ask God for help in our lives, just like you kids ask *me* for help. When we get confused and scared and don't know what to do, God is there to help us. So, when we pray, we are really asking God to help. And just like most dads, God helps His children."

Captivated by what Dad had just said, Jackie sat on his knee and David knelt down at his feet. They wanted to hear more. As she snuggled next to him, Jackie asked, "Does God hear *all* of our prayers?"

"Yes. He does."

"*All* of them?" she questioned again, surprised.

"Yes, all of them," he assured her.

"Wow, that's a lot of prayers."

"Yes it is, but God loves us very much; that's why He listens and answers all of them."

Completely interested in this conversation, David chimed in. "Does He answer all of them *Himself*?"

As the question hung in the air, a smile graced Dad's lips, and a knowing look appeared in his eyes; his demeanor became one of conviction. I was about to find out that he had a deep personal belief in the answer - a belief he had kept to himself for a long time, a belief he had never shared with anyone but was about to share with his family. He looked at each of us and cleared his throat.

"Yes, God hears and answers all our prayers, but He can do it in different ways! Sometimes God answers our prayers directly, Himself. He puts the answer right into our heart, and suddenly, in our own mind, we know what the answer to the prayer is.

"Sometimes the answers come from where we least expect it. There are times when God is very busy," he continued, "and although he hears your prayer, He does not answer it directly or even right away. That's when He answers your prayer through someone else or something else. The answer to your prayer may come through your friend, your mom, your brother, your teacher...you know what I mean? Maybe you asked God for help, and some person said something that made you feel better or made your fears go away. Sometimes God answers our prayers by making something happen. Has that ever happened to you? Have you ever prayed for something and then it happened? Your prayer was answered? "

Jackie turned to face him directly, a questioning look on her face, and asked, "Like when Karen Foley used to make fun of me at school? I prayed to God to make her stop and the next day I found out that she was moving to Florida."

"Well, something like that," Dad chuckled and nodded his head.

The entire family was now completely engrossed and leaned in closer to him so that they would not miss a single word.

"Sometimes the people we care about die. We can't see them anymore and miss them...and when we pray, God answers our prayers through them. This is God's way of keeping us close to them."

He paused for a long moment, and then quietly began again. "I remember one time when I was little, my father got home from work, and as soon as he walked in the door, he knelt down and started to pray. When I asked him why he was praying in the doorway, he told me that he prayed to God because he was worried about his job. The bosses were firing a lot of people and he was afraid that he would lose his job and not be able to take care of his family. I saw him pray several times that night, and the next morning I heard him tell my mother that he'd had a dream. In his dream, my dad's favorite cousin, who had recently died, spoke to my dad and told him not to worry about work, He told him that God

Himself had told him that my dad shouldn't worry about his job because everything was going to be okay. And it was. He didn't lose his job and was able to continue to take care of his family."

"Is that true?" I asked, with the amazed exuberance of a child.

"True story, one hundred percent," he replied.

Looking as though she had just made a discovery, Jackie added. "Wow, God is even cooler than Santa!"

Dad leaned in closer to her, and whispered, "Even Santa works for God."

Dad let that statement sit with her for a moment and then continued. "Sometimes you have to wait a while before your prayer gets answered. That's when we need to be strong, continue to pray, and not give up. We are all God's children, and he wants all of us to share in His love together. I want you to remember that God does listen to us and He does hear our prayers. And although our prayers may be answered in different ways, the answers come from God— always from God."

Illuminated by Dad's passionate account, my brother, sister, and I left our parents and headed off to bed. I could still hear them talking however, and what I overheard impacted me almost as much as what he had said to us directly.

"Wow Anthony! That was some explanation. How did you come up with all of that so quickly?"

"It's not just an explanation. I believe that with all my heart."

"And your father...that part was true?"

"Yep, it's true," he answered, as his thoughts drifted towards his father. "Although I was little when that happened, he and I talked about it just a few weeks before he died. It's funny...it's the last conversation I remember having with him. It was as if he was preparing me for when he would be gone."

"You never told me."

"Come to think of it, I've never told anyone. Until now."

# CHAPTER 15

# DECEMBER 1, 1977

ALTHOUGH THE CATHOLIC SCHOOLS DID NOT HAVE football teams, they *did* have basketball teams. The teams were divided by grades, one through eight, and played in the Catholic Youth Organization (CYO) of New York City. In 1977, my friends and I played on the eighth-grade team.

As we entered the gym on a chilly December afternoon, we were immediately hit by a familiar smell: The gym floor had just been painted with a protective coat of clear varnish that had a distinctive odor. My friends and I stood in a line, breathing in and out to soak up the smell of the varnish.

We were suddenly jolted from our breathing exercises by the shouts of our coach, Mr. Henley.

"What is this, a chorus line? Let's get moving, line up!"

The gym was crowded and loud as our team practiced. We were surrounded by other teams from our school, also at practice. The cheerleaders were on one side of the gym and the drama club on the stage behind us. We heard the loud instructions of the drama teacher and the louder chants of the cheerleaders, but no one could out yell Mr. Henley, who had honed his screaming skills over his twenty-year career as a Marine Drill Sergeant.

"Let's go boys!! Let's get the lead out!! Start moving!!" he screamed, while clapping his hands.

John and I stood on the end of the "pass and shoot" drill line, waiting our turn and fervently hoping that today would not be the day that we became deaf.

"Hey! You going to the party tomorrow?" John practically shouted, although he was standing next to me.

"Yeah, it should be cool."

I was just about to ask him a question when the ball was flipped to me and it was my turn to do the drill. I passed the ball below the basket and then ran behind a screen set by a teammate. Getting the ball at the top of the key, I fired a shot that passed smoothly through the hoop. In my head, I heard legendary New York Knicks broadcaster Marv Albert shout, "Yes!" I ran back and took my place in line.

John joined me after his turn and so I asked him, "Do you know if Lauren is going to the party?"

"Why? Are you *interested* in Lauren?" A huge, devious grin grew on his face.

"I'm not. I was just curious."

"Just curious?"

I realized that I shouldn't have asked about Lauren, so I quickly turned away, trying not to appear interested in his answer. However, we were best friends; there was no way he was going to let me off that easy.

"Look, everyone knows! She knows! You know! So what's the problem?"

I was startled by this declaration. "What do you mean *everyone* knows? Knows *what*?"

"Come on, you guys have been giving each other the "googly" eyes since you were seven years old. Why don't you just kiss her and get it over with?"

"I don't want to kiss her!"

"Oh, sure you don't."

"I don't! And don't go telling anyone that I do!"

He gave me that devious grin again, but didn't say anything else.

And practice continued.

During a scrimmage, a pass flew over my head towards the sideline. I ran to retrieve the rolling ball. As I bent down to pick it up, it was stopped by a foot—the foot of a cheerleader, with white shoes and white ankle socks. I looked up. It was Lauren.

For a moment, I was back on that curb the very first time I met her. I hadn't seen her much recently. She had changed. She didn't look like a little girl anymore. She didn't look like the friend I played catch with. She looked grown up and more beautiful than ever before. My heart began pounding loudly. I hoped no one could hear it. My whole body stirred. I think I was actually trembling a bit. I couldn't stop looking at her. I managed to pick up the ball and we shared an awkward "hello".

Walking back to my practice, I realized how much I missed her. I missed our walks…and we hadn't been to the roof in months.

When practiced ended, the players and cheerleaders mingled about, planning for the weekend ahead. I was talking to a friend by the front door when Lauren approached.

"Hi," she said, quickly looking down.

The best I could do was to mumble a simple "hi" in response.

The awkwardness was back.

I somehow managed to find my voice and asked "Is your mother picking you up or are you walking home?"

"Walking."

"Oh, okay," I muttered.

Suddenly panicked, I began to turn toward my friends but something soft touched my arm. I looked down and saw her hand.

"You want to walk home with me?" she asked, looking vulnerable.

I tried not to seem excited. "Yeah sure … just let me tell John."

As I walked over to him, I just knew he was going to give me grief—given our earlier conversation. "Got a minute?" I asked, as I led him away from the group. "I'm going to walk home with Lauren."

He smiled and I braced for his answer. "Umm..." he started to speak but quickly stopped. I looked at him, and saw that he wasn't smirking.

He just smiled. "Sure, I'll talk to you later."

He understood.

There's nothing like having a best friend.

Lauren and I left the gym. The sky was dark and the air was clear and crisp with the sweet smell of wood burning from the fireplaces of the houses we passed. We walked side by side, struggling with what to say. I know we both purposely walked slowly, trying to delay our arrival home. We walked for about two minutes before either of us spoke at all. I was trying to understand why talking to each other had become so difficult, but finally a "safe" thought entered my mind.

"Hey, my uncle got me tickets for the KISS concert at Madison Square Garden, opening night. December 14th."

Relieved that we were talking, she replied happily, "Wow, that's great. Who's going?"

"John, Steve, Andy, Tony, Tommy, and me."

"You're all going alone?"

"No, my dad is taking us."

We continued to walk, and the silence resumed for a while. Luckily a "safe" thought entered Lauren's head and she broke the silence. "I heard that KISS is going to be on TV in January."

I was surprised that she knew. "Yes, January 10<sup>th</sup> on NBC. Some show called *The Land of Hype and Glory*. It should be cool."

Suddenly, I wanted to talk about what was going on between us: Why we hadn't spoken to each other; why we always seemed to be avoiding each other. I also wanted to tell her how much she meant to me, that I thought about her all the time and that she was the most beautiful girl I had ever seen.

That's what I wanted to talk about, but that's not what came out of my mouth.

"You going to the party on Friday?"

"Yes."

I was unsure, but had to ask.

"Well...if you're not going with anyone, would you like to go with me?"

Before I knew it, we had arrived at the corner of our street. She stopped walking, and stood at the side of a large tree. The Christmas lights of the surrounding houses created a soft colorful glow around her, and I thought that she looked even more beautiful than she had in the gym. She gradually stepped towards me ... and suddenly we were face to face. It wasn't until her lips touched mine that I realized what was happening. All sorts of thoughts raced through my mind, but the important one stood out:

*"I'm kissing Lauren!"*

I was unsure of what to do. I started to put my arms around her, but when they touched her, I quickly brought them back to my side. The kiss lasted for about twenty seconds, and as we moved apart, my thoughts continued racing through my head.

"*What do I do now?*" I was almost panic-stricken, and I could feel my body begin to shake.

"I'm sorry," Lauren said, "but I've wanted to do that for a long time."

My whole body trembled slightly, and my stomach was definitely in a knot, but somehow I managed to answer calmly, "Oh, that's okay. I've thought about it a few times too."

And then the atmosphere between us changed as I looked deeply into her eyes. I instantly knew where I belonged. I felt alive and safe, and the uneasy feeling of the last few months faded away. We had struggled to find the words, but now they were no longer necessary. The comfort that we had always felt with each other was back.

I wanted to kiss her again and stepped towards her. Just then, a car came around the corner—its headlights shining on us. We moved away from each other and watched the car as it faded from view.

The moment had passed.

She stepped back. "Well…I guess I'll see you at school."

"Yeah, I'll see you tomorrow."

We walked side by side for about twenty feet, then she veered left towards her house and I veered right towards mine. I turned my head to look back at her, and at the same time, she glanced back at me. We smiled at each other and I knew.

No one else in the world knew. But I knew.

We would always be together.

# Chapter 16

# A Month to Remember

I left Lauren and walked into my house through the garage, where I dropped off my basketball equipment. In the kitchen, I had opened the refrigerator to look for a drink when my mom came in. "Hi Michael! So tell me ... how was practice?"

"Good," I answered quickly, trying to head off to my bedroom.

"Are you hungry? Shall I make you something to eat?"

"No. Thank you. I'm fine."

I reached my bedroom and quickly closed the door behind me. I sat on my bed for a while then decided to call John. I dialed the first few numbers and then hung up. A few moments later, I dialed again and hung up again. I think I was a little nervous. I had to tell someone though, so I dialed again and this time waited until John picked up.

"John, guess what?"

"What?"

"I kissed Lauren."

"No way! I was only kidding at the gym!"

"Yes way! I did it!"

"Oh man! ... How was it?"

"It was good ... felt a little weird, but good."

"This is huge!"

"I know."

Lying in bed that night, I thought of what had happened between Lauren and me that day. The kiss had brought us back together.

I couldn't wait to see her again.

I sat up in bed and looked over to my desk; the desk light was still on, making the small calendar in the corner stand out. I walked to the desk, sat down, and reached for it. The first thing I noticed was the date. I stared at it for a while, then grabbed a pen and tenderly wrote "Lauren" in the box.

When I was done, I glanced out my bedroom window. It had started to snow and I silently watched the snowflakes fall gracefully to the ground below.

Later on, I lay in bed staring at the ceiling for the longest time...but I felt peaceful and contented.

It was December 1, 1977.

I finally fell asleep.

I didn't know it at the time, but December of 1977 would be a month filled with events that I would remember for the rest of my life.

# Chapter 17

# The Next Day and Twelve Days

THE NEXT MORNING, I TRUDGED THROUGH THE SNOW with John to the school-bus stop. Several of our friends were already there. Andy stepped in front of me when we joined them, his eyes wide with excitement. "Oh man, you kissed Lauren!"

I was shocked. "How do *you* know?"

Andy looked at John, who tried to look away.

"Thanks for keeping it a secret," I said sarcastically. John started to say something but was interrupted.

"What secret?" Steve added knowingly. "Everybody *knew* this would happen."

I was then inundated with questions from my curious friends.

"How was it?" Tony asked first.

"Good."

"How long did you kiss her for?" Steve chimed in.

"I don't know ... twenty seconds maybe."

"How many times?" Tommy wanted to know.

"Just once."

"Did you French kiss her?" Tony asked in a whisper.

I didn't know what Tony was talking about. I had no idea what the French were doing. I was nervous enough just doing it the American way. But there was only one answer I could give:

"Yeah, of course."

The entire group took a step back as though I had performed some kind of miracle.

"That is *soooo* cool!" Tommy exclaimed.

Luckily, the bus arrived, putting an end to the assault of questions, but my head was reeling. When the bus pulled away, I leaned over to John and whispered in his ear, "What's a French kiss?"

He shrugged, so I guess he didn't know either.

I got off the bus in a daze and walked into school. I saw Lauren briefly at the bus stop, but didn't really have a chance to talk to her…and I wouldn't until later in the day.

The first five periods of the school day dragged on and I don't think I really heard anything that any of my teachers said. I kept thinking of Lauren and what had passed between us the night before. I walked down the hall with my friends towards my sixth-period Religion class, not engaging in the conversation that surrounded me. Religion was the only class that Lauren and I had together, and the anticipation of seeing her had built up all day.

When I entered the classroom, I immediately looked to her seat. She was there. She stood up when I got to her. I couldn't help staring into her eyes.

"I missed you," I said, without thinking.

"I missed you too," she said softly.

And we just stood there, alone for a moment, just staring into each other's eyes.

Suddenly, I had a feeling that something was not quite right, so I slowly turned around...and noticed that the entire class was staring at us. Like it or not, we were going to be that day's gossip.

Fortunately, my embarrassment was short lived as Father Valenti entered the room and quickly brought the class to attention. Father Valenti's classes were always interesting, because they were more like discussions than lectures.

"Okay, okay ... everyone take your seat as we have little to do and a lot of time to do it." His mistake hung in the air for a few seconds before scattered giggles filled the classroom.

"All right, give me a break; it's been a rough day."

The room settled down as Father Valenti moved to the front of his desk and leaned against it.

"Today is December 2nd" he began, "and there are only twenty-three days left until Christmas. So, today's discussion will focus on a particular part of Christmas, and enhance your knowledge of Christmas traditions. Hopefully, what you learn today will help you enjoy this Christmas season a little bit more. So let's start with a question: What makes Christmas memorable or special for you?"

The hand of a pretty, red-haired girl in the front of the class shot up. "Christmas presents!" she announced happily.

"Christmas presents," Father Valenti repeated. "Okay, that's a good one. Anyone else?" He looked around for other volunteers. Several hands shot up in the air and Father Valenti pointed to them one at a time. "Jimmy what about you?"

"My family only bakes special cakes and cookies at Christmas time , so that's memorable."

"That's good! Good!...Vincent, your turn."

"Being with my entire family! My family lives all over the country, so at Christmas my whole family gets together. *All* my aunts, uncles, and cousins!"

"Also very good!" Father Valenti smiled. "Anyone else?"

From the corner of my eye, I saw Lauren raise her hand.

"Yes, Lauren?"

"Christmas carols."

"Ah! Christmas carols. Yes! As a young boy nothing made me feel the Christmas spirit as much as Christmas carols. I loved singing them and I loved hearing them."

Nodding heads and murmurs of agreement filled the classroom.

"Any personal favorites?" Father Valenti asked.

"*Jingle Bells!*" a voice from the back shouted.

"*White Christmas!*"

"*The First Noel!*"

"*The Little Drummer Boy!*"

"*Rudolph, The Red-Nosed Reindeer!*"

"*Frosty the Snowman!*"

Father Valenti raised his hands and the class quickly settled down.

"All the songs you mentioned are wonderful, beautiful songs ... and Christmas wouldn't be the same without them." He moved toward the blackboard and grabbed a piece of chalk. "But there is another song I want to talk about today. How many of you know '*The Twelve Days of Christmas?*' " He wrote the name of the song on the board.

Everyone raised their hands. I wondered why he wanted to talk about this particular song.

"Okay, okay ... you all know the song," he said, acknowledging all the hands up in the air. "But do you know the origins of the song or its true meaning?"

"I know," said a girl in the front row. "It's about giving presents on the twelve days before Christmas."

"Well," Father Valenti said, smiling gently, "actually it's not." He walked over to a large calendar that hung on the wall. "The twelve days actually refer to the days between December 25th and the Epiphany on January 6th. The Epiphany, also known as 'Little Christmas', is recognized as the day the three kings arrived with gifts for the baby Jesus."

A wave of anticipation swept the room as we all wondered what was to follow. Father Valenti moved back behind his desk, reached for a piece of paper, and began to read, "As for each individual day and what each gift symbolizes, the code for each gift dates back to the time when Catholics were not allowed to openly celebrate their religion in England.

So, as a means to both celebrate and pass on their religious beliefs to their children, Catholics composed and began singing *The Twelve Days of Christmas*, with each gift bearing some religious significance."

The classroom was still as he continued.

"The song is a reflection of the love between Catholics and God. 'My true love' refers to God and 'me' refers to the Catholics. Would you like to hear what the twelve gifts actually represent?"

We all shouted, "Yes!"

He walked over to a separate, covered chalkboard, and lifted the cover.

"Okay, so here it is," he said, and pointed to a list he had previously written:

- A Partridge in a Pear Tree: Jesus Christ, the son of God

- Two Turtle Doves: the Old and New Testament

- Three French Hens: the virtues of Faith, Hope, and Charity

- Four Calling Birds: the four Gospels

- Five Golden Rings: the first five books of the Old Testament, all of which dealt with man's fall from grace

- Six Geese A-Laying: the six days of creation

- Seven Swans A-Swimming: the seven Sacraments

- Eight Maids A-Milking: the eight Beatitudes

- Nine Ladies Dancing: the nine fruits of the Holy Spirit

- Ten Lords A-Leaping: the Ten Commandments

- Eleven Pipers Piping: the eleven faithful apostles (excluding Judas)

- Twelve Drummers Drumming: the twelve points of doctrine in the Apostle's Creed

He paused, allowing us to digest all this information, and then he slowly walked back to his desk and sat down. "Any questions?"

Dozens of hands flew up. He smiled, contentedly thinking, *"This is why you teach."*

He answered all of our questions and the class flew by. Just as it was ending, he grew serious and began, "Today we touched on many things about Christmas, and all of it is good, but don't ever forget that the most important part of Christmas is really the birth of Jesus Christ. This is what Christmas is all about! All of the other things about Christmas are great—the presents, your family, the food, the lights, the carols, and the Christmas trees. These are all wonderful things and you should enjoy them. But all of that pales in comparison to the birth of Jesus Christ and what his birth meant, *and* still means, to the world. No man in history has had a more profound impact on the world than Christ.

"So enjoy this Christmas season. Enjoy all of it ... but remember, as with all things, to always keep Christ in the center of your lives."

# Chapter 18

# December 3, 1977
# The First Game

It was a frosty and sunny Saturday morning. John and I arrived at the football field at around 9:30 for the first game of the tournament, between St. Patrick and St. Thomas. It was hard to believe that just a week ago we had kicked off this tournament with the meeting.

We climbed the steps of the bleachers that surrounded the sideline, stopped halfway to make sure we had a good view of the field, and sat to watch the teams as they ran various drills and warmed up for the game.

"What do you think?" John asked after we had watched for about ten minutes.

"St. Thomas," I responded confidently." Too big... too strong."

"Yeah, but they're slow."

I smiled. "Trust me, St. Thomas will win."

Before long we were joined by the other team captains. We exchanged quick greetings, but avoided any prolonged conversation as we were totally in game mode.

The game started and each team began probing for the other's weaknesses. From the beginning, St. Thomas ran the ball against the smaller St. Patrick team. St. Thomas scored two touchdowns to take a 14-0 halftime lead.

The second half was a repeat of the first. St. Thomas threw only five passes the entire game. They continued to pound the ball at the St. Patrick team and beat them decisively:

St. Thomas-35

St. Patrick-14

"That was impressive." I said quietly to John.

"Yeah, they looked good," he replied, a hint of worry in his voice.

As we sat on the bleachers talking about the next game, Bobby Ross walked onto the field to warm up.

"Hey, Ross!" I called out, and waited for him to turn around.

He scanned the bleachers and quickly spotted me.

"Don't let me down!" I shouted.

He smiled back confidently, put his helmet on, and ran off.

Bobby didn't let anyone down. He was amazing. He scored five touchdowns. On two of the runs, it seemed as though he went through the entire defense. Then the game was over.

St. Charles-42

Our Lady Star of the Sea-7

St. Charles and Bobby were even better than we thought.

After the game, Bobby stopped at the bleachers, removed his helmet, and looked up to where I was sitting. I waited for an "I told you so." It never came. Instead, he hollered, "Good luck later!" and smiled warmly.

"Thanks!" I called back, slightly surprised.

In the third game, St. Teresa defeated Our Lady Queen of Peace, 21-14.

The fourth and last game of the day was ours: Holy Child versus St. Clare. We warmed up on opposite sides of the field. As we ran through our drills, we loudly chanted our mantra: "Nothing more! Nothing less! Nothing more! Nothing less! Nothing more! Nothing less!"

The chant had started one day at practice back in October. Our team had been standing in a circle discussing plans for practice, when Tommy, who was a few minutes late, jogged over, excited and slightly out of breath.

"I thought of a slogan for the team when I was in class today!...so, I'm sitting in science class and suddenly this phrase just popped into my head. 'We want nothing more and we will accept nothing less.' Get it? 'We want nothing more than the championship and we will accept nothing less than the championship.'"

Tony immediately approved. "That's good. That's really good."

I'd liked it, but wasn't completely sold. "Yeah, it's good... but it's too long."

John had then stepped into the middle of the circle and offered an alternative: "How about, 'Nothing more! Nothing less!'?"

"That's it! That's great!" Steve shouted. We agreed immediately, moving closer into the circle, enthusiastically jumping up and down while we chanted, "Nothing more! Nothing less! Nothing more! Nothing less! Nothing more! Nothing less!"

The warm up was over. We lost the toss, and kicked-off to St. Clare to start the game.

St. Clare received the kick and returned the ball to their 25-yard line. I called the team together into the huddle.

"Okay, guys. Standard 4-3 defense. Let's give them nothing."

"No way can they move the ball on us," John said, as he jumped up and down.

"Let's set the tone right away."

The teams broke their huddles; the players from each team eyed each other, looking to intimidate, and took their positions. The quarterback barked out the signals.

"Ready, set...hut one, hut two ..." The ball was snapped. The quarterback turned to his right and pitched the ball to the running back. The back received the ball. After two steps, he was met and stopped by four members of our defense. We jumped up and congratulated each other. St. Clare ran two more plays that gained them only five yards. St. Clare punted the ball on fourth down. The ball was received and returned to the Holy Child 40-yard line. Our offense huddled up.

John, our quarterback, entered the huddle and immediately took control.

"We're going for it right away. Right receiver streak on one."

I was the right receiver, and as we broke the huddle, John and I smiled at each other. It was a play we had run thousands of times in the street, the schoolyard, and at practice. John set the offense, looked at the defense, and then quickly called the play: "Ready, set, hut!"

The ball was snapped and John took a quick drop. He looked at Tommy, the left receiver, pumping the ball to momentarily freeze the defense, quickly turned back to the right, and without looking, threw a long pass to where he knew I would be. The ball flew through the air in a perfect spiral, and began coming down after forty yards. I was now at full speed, with the defender three yards behind me, as the ball dropped softly into my hands. Untouched, I ran the rest of the way for a touchdown.

The entire team ran to the end zone to congratulate me. As I was coming out of the end zone, John was just getting there. "Great throw," I said and extended my hand.

He grabbed it and pulled me close. "Nice catch."

As the game continued, it became apparent that we were too strong for the St. Clare team. By the end of the third quarter, the score was 27-0. John called the team together. "No more scoring. Just goal-line dives."

A few of our players were unhappy, because they wanted to continue scoring. John quickly put them in their place, shouting into their faces. "Hey! No more! We will do this the right way."

The final score was 27-0. The two teams mingled on the field and shook hands, offering each other congratulations and condolences.

*"One game down, and two to go"* I thought, as I walked off the field ... knowing that the next game would be much tougher.

# Chapter 19

# Love

The kiss brought Lauren and me back together. We spent the next week catching up on all that we had missed over the previous few months. It was great talking to her and I felt like we were little kids again. We talked about the upcoming holidays, and asked each other what we wanted for Christmas. One night, after finishing my homework, I called her and asked if she wanted to go for a walk. She was excited and met me outside. As usual, our walk led us to the roof.

It had snowed during the day, and when we reached the top, we were stunned by the intense beauty around us. The colorful lights on the houses bounced off the snow and created a dazzling rainbow of vibrant hues. I took Lauren's hand in mine and led her to the bench, where we sat down.

We admired the beauty of the scene below us and I slowly put my arm around her. Our eyes met. I didn't know what it was that I was feeling at that moment; I just knew that I had never felt anything like it before.

"What do you think about when we come up here?" she asked.

"Nothing."

"I'm serious," she persisted. "What do you think about?"

"I'm serious too." I answered, turning towards her.

"I never think of anything when I'm with you."

"Um...what's that supposed to mean?"

"No, no," I said, momentarily flustered. "What I mean is... um...well, when I'm with you, I really don't think of anything else. You know, it's weird. When I'm at school, or with my friends, or when I watch TV, I can think of other things, and my mind can wander off to some other place. But when I'm with you ... I don't think of anything *but* you."

She leaned in close to me. "That's really, really sweet. Thank you." Then she gently laid her hand on my cheek, and kissed me softly. A moment later she pulled back and looked at me...sort of sadly.

"What's the matter?" I asked.

"Nothing."

I could sense that she wanted to say something else.

"C'mon, you can tell me."

"It's nothing ... really."

She was clearly lying and her tone was so melancholy that I couldn't let it drop. "Lauren, please...tell me what's wrong."

I noticed tears running down her face, but before I could say anything else, she started to explain. "I missed you so much when we weren't talking. I thought about you all the time...and I was scared that we would never be close again."

Her words startled me, and for a moment I didn't know what to say. I wanted to say something perfect, but instead I just I said what I felt. "I missed you too. The whole time we didn't see each other, or even talk to each other...I still felt you around me. I was scared too, but I always felt you in my heart."

She smiled at me and laid her head on my shoulder.

I was silent, but the voice in my head whispered, "*I love you.*"

# Chapter 20

# December 10, 1977
# The Second Game

I got up early, because I couldn't really sleep. I opened my bedroom window and the biting cold hit me. My breath formed clouds in the air. I turned on the radio just in time to hear the DJ happily announce that the current temperature was "twenty-two degrees with a wind chill factor of ten degrees".

"Ahhh...the cold," I muttered, as I pulled on my jersey. "Perfect weather for a football game." The doorbell rang and I quickly ran down the stairs to the door. I looked through the little window at the top of it and saw John. He practically jumped through the doorway when I opened it.

"Oh man is it cold!!" he said, and shook himself to get warm. He was fully dressed, in his football uniform and helmet, and carried a football in his hand. He wasn't wearing a jacket.

"You're dressed already?"

"I've been up since 5:30...couldn't sleep ...too excited."

I headed back upstairs. "I gotta get ready. Get yourself something to eat if you want."

"Are you kidding? If I eat anything, I'll throw up."

We arrived at the field only a few minutes before the first game of the day. We tried to sit in the stands but quickly thought better of it as the steel benches were just way too cold.

The first game was between St. Charles and St. Thomas, and standing on the sideline, I searched for Bobby Ross and spotted him.

"Does Ross look even bigger than usual?"

John turned, looked at Bobby, and then looked at me warily.

"No, he looks the same. You know, I'm starting to worry about you. You spend too much time thinking about him."

"Excuse me for worrying! He's only the best player out here."

He wasn't convinced. "You worry too much," he smirked. "Maybe we'll get lucky and they'll lose today...and if they win, maybe we'll get lucky and *we'll* lose."

I smiled at John with a sarcastic warning look that said, "We better not lose."

"Hey you never know!," he said, smiling. "I'm the quarterback, and I don't want to face that lunatic. Maybe I'll throw the game."

"You do that and *I'll* kill ya!"

We both laughed as the game began.

St. Charles received the opening kick-off, returning the ball to their 35-yard line. On first down, they ran a sweep to the left to Bobby Ross. He gained twenty-five yards. The next play was also a sweep to the left to Ross—this time for thirty yards. The next play was a repeat of the previous two, and this time Ross jogged into the end zone untouched.

St. Charles-7

St.Thomas-0

Worried, I turned to John, "Wow! Three plays, sixty-five yards, and he wasn't even touched until he hit the secondary. They look good."

"All right ... so they can run the ball. Still haven't seen if they can throw it," John said, trying not to seem concerned.

I was still worried. "They run like that ... they won't *have* to throw."

"Well, I'm not worried," John added confidently.

"Well, I'm glad you're not."

St. Thomas got the ball. After just one first down they were forced to punt. The St. Charles offense moved up to the line of scrimmage with their quarterback barking out the count. He dropped back and completed a pass to the wide receiver, cutting over the middle for a large gain. On the next play, the wide receiver ran a deep pattern down the right sideline. The pass was perfectly thrown for a touchdown and a 13-0 lead. The extra point was good.

St. Charles-14

St. Thomas-0

"Now I'm worried," John said, his confidence gone.

"Oh, don't worry," I teased. "They're not as good as they look."

St. Thomas was a tough team, but they just couldn't do enough to score and the first half ended with the score 14-0 in St Charles' favor.

At the start of the second half, St. Thomas caught a break. St. Charles fumbled deep in their territory. St. Thomas struck quickly on a well-executed screen play, and after the extra point, the score was 14-7.

"We got a game!" I said excitedly, and proceeded to "punch" John in the arm.

"Yes, we do! We got a game here!"

St. Charles received the kick-off and returned the ball to their 20-yard line. They went back to the running game. Ross continued to run sweeps left and right for large gains. After six plays, St. Charles had a first and goal on the 3-yard line.

First down: Ross straight ahead to the right of the center - no gain.

Second down: Ross straight ahead to the left of the center - no gain.

Third down: Ross straight ahead, right behind the center - no gain.

Fourth down: Ross on a sweep left - walks into the end zone untouched.

Touchdown!

... and an instant discovery for me.

"Did you see that John?" I asked, hoping that he did.

He nodded, "I saw that!" He totally understood what had just happened.

A huge grin appeared on my face. "They can't run inside!"

"They can't run inside," John agreed, still nodding. "Their center is weak. That's it! That's the spot! We can't let Ross get wide on us!"

St. Thomas tried to come back, but a late interception return for a touchdown sealed their fate.

St. Charles-28

St. Thomas-7

Our game was up next and our team began warm-ups. Halfway through, John called the team to huddle up. When we were together, he looked at each player and spoke. "St. Teresa picked the wrong team to play today. If we do what we're supposed to do, no way they beat us. Do all the little things right. Be smart; be tough; no one can 'beat beat us. Remember: 'Nothing more! Nothing less! Nothing more! Nothing less!' "

That was enough to get us going. The entire team moved together, jumping up and down and chanting loudly: "Nothing more! Nothing less! Nothing more! Nothing less!"

The game began. Each team had the ball twice but was unable to gain any significant yardage. With one minute to go in the half, and the ball at midfield, St. Teresa ran a halfback option. The ball was pitched to the halfback as he ran to his right. He stopped suddenly and prepared to throw. He threw a long pass across the field. Our safety, drawn in by the hand off, scrambled back to the receiver. He was too late. The ball arrived a second before he reached the receiver. The ball was caught on the 5-yard line and run in for a touchdown. The extra point was good.

St. Teresa-7

Holy Child-0

We got the ball back. On first down, John dropped back to pass and was hit from the blind side. He fumbled the ball. St. Teresa recovered on the 15-yard line. There was time left for only one play. St. Teresa elected for a field goal. The kick was good and the half ended with the score:

St. Teresa-10

Holy Child-0

We walked slowly and dejectedly to the end zone for the half-time break. For the longest time, no one spoke. Suddenly, I stood up and the words just came out. "This is my fault," I said, looking around the group. "I spent so much time talking about Ross and St. Charles, and telling you guys that we could beat them, that I didn't concentrate enough on just winning *this* game first." I tried to look each of them in the eye. "I'm sorry."

I could feel the mood change.

John stood up. "This is my fault. I shouldn't have fumbled."

A second later, Steve stood. "This is my fault. I didn't block the guy who hit John."

Then Tommy got up. "This is my fault. I dropped a pass that would have been a first down."

And so it continued. One by one, each member of the team stood up and admitted their mistakes. The whole team stood…together.

And we knew we would win.

We could feel it.

John looked at me. "We're ready."

"Let's go get them!" I roared.

Tommy began shouting: "Nothing more! Nothing less! Nothing more! Nothing less!"

The team came together, formed a circle around Tommy, and joined in, chanting at the top of their lungs: "Nothing more! Nothing less! Nothing more! Nothing less! Nothing more! Nothing less!"

St. Teresa never knew what hit them.

We scored the first four times we had the ball in the second half, and never allowed St. Teresa past midfield. We scored again late in the game and won convincingly:

**Holy Child-35**

**St. Teresa-10**

Now we were ready to play St. Charles. Now we knew we could win.

I once heard it said that no accomplishments are so great as those that are accomplished with others.

I never felt closer to my friends.

# Chapter 21

# December 14, 1977
# Back in the New York Groove

The night had finally arrived.

By the time KISS came to New York for their three sold-out concerts at Madison Square Garden, they were the biggest band on the planet. In the previous two years, they had recorded four albums, all of which reached platinum status. They had just returned from Japan, where they had done five shows at Tokyo's famed Budokan, eclipsing the record held by The Beatles. They were on the cover of virtually every music magazine in America and would be featured in an upcoming NBC news special, *The Land of Hype and Glory* with Edwin Newman. Merchandising was unlike any other band: there were KISS T-shirts, posters, dolls, photos, belt buckles, and a special kit for joining the Kiss Army. They had won the People's Choice Award for their single *"Beth"*. They had a comic book and would soon have a made-for-TV movie. They were named "America's Favorite Rock Group" in a Gallup poll of teens.

Much to my father's relief, there had been a change in his work schedule, so Uncle Rich volunteered to take us to the concert in his place. That night, my friends and I waited outside my house for Uncle Rich to pick us up. We were overly excited and time seemed to move too slowly—as it always seems to do when you're waiting for something really important to happen.

It felt like I had waited a lifetime to see KISS in concert and I was only thirteen!

I turned to Andy. "Oh man, I can't wait! This is gonna be awesome!"

Andy started announcing, in a loud, deep bass voice: "YOU WANTED THE BEST!" Everyone joined in with the thunderous response: "YOU GOT THE BEST! THE HOTTEST BAND IN THE WORLD!...KISSSS!!"

"I hope they open with '*Detroit Rock City*," Tommy said.

"I don't think so," John chimed in. "I heard that they're opening with '*I Stole Your Love*."

"I don't care what they open with," Steve said. "Whatever it is, it's gonna be unbelievable!"

We continued to talk about the KISS rumors we'd heard on the radio, when a familiar car turned the corner. It was Uncle Rich, triggering enthusiastic cheers from our group. He parked the car and walked up the driveway, laughing at us as we performed our own air-guitar concert. My mother met him at the top of the driveway, as we flew past him and into the car.

"You're crazy to do this, Rich," she said.

"Yeah," he grinned. "Isn't my brother supposed to do these things?"

"Your brother is more than happy to let *you* do this one."

"I'm sure he is."

"It's going to be very loud you know ... and you'll be the oldest person there."

"I know, I know ... but I promised," he said kindly. "Well, we better get going. We don't want to be late." He said goodbye and made his way back to his car.

There was a growing sense of excitement and anticipation as we drove into Manhattan. We drifted in and out of conversations as each of us imagined what we were about to see. Going to your very first concert is quite an amazing experience. Seeing your favorite band for that first time happens only once. KISS was the biggest band on the planet. Their concerts were legendary...and soon we would be right smack in the middle of one.

We exited the Brooklyn Battery Tunnel and stopped at a light across the street from the World Trade Center, admiring the sheer size of the towers. We continued driving through the west side of Manhattan until we reached 34th Street, and parked in the garage around the corner from Madison Square Garden. We walked down 34th Street until we reached 8th Avenue, and when we turned the corner, "The Garden" was in sight.

A huge KISS ARMY flag hung from the top of the building, and a large, electronic sign that read: "KISS in Concert Tonight 8:00 p.m." was out front.

We passed through the gate after we presented our tickets, and found ourselves in the concert hall. "Wow! This place is really huge," John said, as we all looked around.

Unable to fully contain our excitement and wonder, we followed Uncle Rich to our seats...and then saw the stage.

We were only a hundred feet away...and the view was perfect.

Uncle Rich had come through *big time.* "These seats are just so great, Uncle Rich! Thanks a lot for getting them!" I said, with unbridled enthusiasm.

"Way to go Uncle Rich!" agreed the others, still staring at the stage.

"You're welcome; you're welcome," he answered, pleased that he had made a bunch of kids so happy, but aware that he was closer than he wanted to be...and that it would be louder than he even cared to think about.

The Garden filled with the song '*Whole Lotta Love*' by Led Zeppelin. When the song ended, the Garden went black... and the crowd exploded with anticipation.

I can still see the entire concert in my mind's eye, as if it were happening all over again:

A dull, deep bass chord fills the arena …

Lights flash throughout the arena ...

A smashing guitar chord rocks the arena ...

A ten-second pounding of drums beats through the arena ...

The anticipation builds up in the arena ...

Just when it seems that the night will never begin, a voice cracks through the arena ...

"ALL RIGHT NEW YORK! YOU WANTED THE BEST! YOU GOT THE BEST! THE HOTTEST BAND IN THE WORLD...KIIIIISSSSS!!!!"

The crowd explodes in a deafening roar. The stage is quickly covered by a layer of thick, liquid fog and smoke, enveloping the drums. Synchronized lights flash across the stage. The drum beats loudly, and the four KISS members suddenly appear. Ace and Paul are in a mechanical box, high above the right side of the stage. Gene is also in a mechanical box, but high to the left. Peter, in the center of the stage, is surrounded by a huge drum kit. The band rips into 'I Stole Your Love.' At the beginning of the song, the mechanical boxes move away from the stage wall, and head on down to the stage floor. The crowd continues to cheer as Gene, Paul, and Ace touch down. The doors of the mechanical boxes fly open and the band members jump out onto the stage.

The stage explodes with fireworks and large bursts of flames. Behind the drums, at the back of the stage, is a towering electric sign with a huge KISS logo that burns throughout the show.

Paul kicks off the night and takes command of the stage, pumping up the crowd as he dances across it. The band members, in their giant platform boots, stand at least seven feet tall, dwarfing the fans below them.

Gene prowls the stage, sneering and constantly sticking his tongue out—to the delight of the crowd. Gene is clearly the main event. During 'God of Thunder', he flicks his tongue and drools fake blood. In the final moments of the song 'Firehouse', he swishes kerosene around in his mouth, holds a lit torch in his hand, sprays the kerosene into the flame, and is suddenly breathing fire.

Ace rocks back and forth throughout the songs. During his solo, his guitar repeatedly appears to catch fire and dense clouds of white smoke and orange sparks can be seen spewing out if it.

Peter sits atop an enormous drum kit. The entire kit moves from front to back and then side to side during his solo. Late in the show, he sits alone on stage ... singing the band's biggest hit, 'Beth', while he hands out roses to the crowd.

The night continues and the band rips through the set list, arriving finally at the last song: 'Black Diamond'.

The stage is completely dark. From the right side of the stage, Paul emerges alone. He stands in front of the microphone, but does not speak. Under a bright purple spotlight, he begins the guitar 'intro' to 'Black Diamond'. When he finishes, exploding fireworks completely illuminate the stage and the entire band kicks into the song.

As the song winds down, Gene, on the left, and Paul and Ace on the right, are lifted above the crowd on platform risers. In the center of the stage, Peter's drum kit is lifted fifty feet above the stage, and below the drums appear two large, gold cats with sparkling red eyes. The platforms are then lowered back to the stage and KISS is back on it. Suddenly, Paul grabs his guitar, steps back, and then lunges forward, smashing it against the stage. It does not break. He smashes it again. It breaks in two. He wraps it up with the guitar strings and throws it to a fan in the crowd. Ace, Gene, and Peter continue to play as Paul reaches for the microphone.

"GOODNIGHT NEW YORK! WE LOVE YOU! SEE YOU SOON!"

The stage explodes in a series of fireworks and confetti. The last chord is struck and the concert is over. We watch as the band walks off the stage. The lights inside the Garden come back on. The stage is now covered with a dense layer of smoke.

It is over.

Silence emanates from the group—the silence that comes from an incredibly awesome experience...an experience that takes one's breath away.

Suddenly, Tommy shouts, "Oh ... My ... God...*THAT* was just *INCREDIBLE!!*"

His voice shook us out of our reverie, and we all shouted at the same time:

"Unbelievable!"

"So cool!"

"Fantastic!"

I summed it up for everyone, I think, when I pronounced it, "Absolutely the greatest night of my life!"

Uncle Rich didn't say anything.

By the time we reached the car we were exhausted, and didn't say much on the ride home. Besides, our ears were ringing!

Dad was waiting up for us. He was already on the driveway when we pulled up. We scrambled out of the car and made our way up the driveway, said 'hello' to him and headed into my house. Dad walked towards Uncle Rich, who was just getting out of his car.

"So, how was it?" he asked Uncle Rich with real curiosity (I guess he knew what *my* answer would be; that's why he asked Uncle Rich first!).

"Oh, it sucked," Uncle Rich answered without hesitation.

"That bad, huh?"

"Actually, it wasn't *that* bad. I mean, yeah, the music sucked, but I have to admit that the show was really cool, and the kids loved it. They don't realize that nobody will even remember KISS five years from now."

"I know. Michael told me the other day that someday he would take his kids to see KISS."

They both laughed at the thought.

"Well, it's late; I guess I should go." Uncle Rich started to leave.

"Hey, Rich?" Dad called out, and Uncle Rich turned to look at him.

"Thanks man."

Uncle Rich smiled back, "No problem, bro."

It was a great night.

# CHAPTER 22

# DECEMBER 16, 1977
## ONE MORE PRACTICE

WE MET AFTER SCHOOL FOR ONE MORE QUICK PRACTICE before the championship game.

After working on some plays we mingled in small groups discussing our strategies. But practice would be over soon as the sun was approaching the horizon, and the field was getting darker.

"I think we're good," Andy said. "We went over all of our offensive and defensive plays. We should be okay."

"Just can't let him get wide," I said about no one in particular, but, of course, it was about Bobby Ross.

Tommy pointed towards me with the football in his hand. "He won't. If he runs, we'll make him pay."

I turned to face Andy and Tommy. "You two guys are the key. If you can turn him inside, into the pursuit, he'll have nowhere to go. If they try to go inside, Steve will destroy that center. Just remember, we have to gang tackle him. He's too strong one on one."

"Speak for yourself!" Steve jumped in, taking offense to what I had said. "He comes anywhere near me and I'm gonna lay him out."

John walked over to me, a look of concern on his face. "Did you see the weather for tonight and tomorrow? Cold and rainy."

"That would be perfect," I said, knowing that bad field conditions could slow Ross down.

"For *defense* it will help. Just remember that *we* have to score too."

"We'll be okay on offense," Andy added. "We can move on them. We're too fast for them."

Practice was just about to break up when John asked, "What about last play options?"

"What?" asked Steve, not understanding the question.

"You know…last play. What if we only have time for one more play? What are we going to run?"

"We'll run a Big Ben or a Hail Mary," Tommy said confidently. "Send everyone deep."

Not quite convinced, John scanned the group. "Everyone think that's okay?"

Everyone agreed except me. "No, that's not good. They'll expect that. They'll just drop everyone back. It won't work."

"Well then, what else?" John asked.

"I remember my dad telling me about a play he saw once, in a college game, for a situation just like that. We can put it in now."

Steve sighed. "Come on. I'm tired, and it's cold."

"Yeah, I'm tired too," Andy agreed. "Let's go."

I never had a chance to answer back or even explain because John jumped in immediately. "Hey! Tomorrow is forever. We have to be ready for anything!"

John's opinion always carried more weight than mine, and the rest of the team stood up. "Okay, let's do it."

John turned and pointed to me, "Okay, you're up."

As I pictured the formation in my head, I started to direct the offense into the positions needed to run the play.

We continued to practice until the sun set completely and the field turned black.

Several times I caught myself thinking back to the phrase that John had spoken earlier. As usual, he was right.

Tomorrow would be forever.

# CHAPTER 23

# IT MEANS EVERYTHING

WE LEFT PRACTICE COLD AND TIRED BUT COMFORTED BY the fact that we had done all we could do to get ready for tomorrow's game.

I removed my uniform in the laundry room and headed for the shower, stopping in the kitchen to say hello to my family. The hot water from the shower felt good as I looked at the bruises that covered my body. I quickly brushed them out of my thoughts, telling myself that there was only one game left to play and I would have plenty of time to rest after that.

After dinner, I spoke very briefly with Andy and John about the game, and then decided not to think about it anymore. I tried to put it out of my mind by watching TV and going to bed early. I lay down on my bed, exhausted both mentally and physically. After an hour of tossing and turning, I was still wide awake and unable to shake the game from my mind. I decided to get up. I walked through the house, careful to be quiet since everyone was asleep, my thoughts loudly racing through my mind. Suddenly, I felt the need to be outside and feel the cold. I dressed quickly and left the house, closing the front door quietly behind me.

I stood outside for a while, circling the driveway as my mind sought some measure of calmness. There was none to be found. Before I knew it, I began walking down the street and quickly found myself at the park. I crouched down and went through the hole in the fence that led directly to the field where tomorrow's game would be played. I viewed the field from one end to the other, and then slowly climbed into the stands.

The field was quiet and I imagined how different it would be tomorrow, during the action of a football game. I thought back to when my friends and I were eight years old and played together for the first time, and how much had changed since then. I was lost in these thoughts when I heard a noise behind me. Startled and scared, I turned abruptly towards the sound and was shocked to see my father emerge from the hole in the fence. I was very relieved to see that it wasn't something else, but worried that he was at the field. I jumped down from the stands.

"Dad, what are you doing here? You can't be here."

"Don't worry; I won't be here for the game."

"You know about the game?" I was stunned.

"Yes, I know about the game."

"Oh no … but parents aren't allowed."

"Relax. No one will know I was here."

"Yeah, but ... wait...how do you know about the game?"

Facing me, Dad laid his hands on my shoulders. "You're my son. Don't ever think for a moment that I don't know what's going on in your life. Being a parent is not just about saying yes or no; it's about being part of your life. It's also about knowing when to be involved and when to step back and let you live your life. Your friends, your team, and the game tomorrow...it's for you. Good or bad, it's yours."

"Then why are you here?"

"Because I know you're scared. I know how much it means to you, John, and all the other guys. I wanted to tell you that, no matter what, you'll be okay."

"It's *not* okay. We have to win. It means everything." I turned away.

"I know it means everything. So do a lot of things. In your lifetime you'll have fifty or sixty moments that mean everything. Some of those moments you'll win, and some you'll lose, but win or lose ... it's all about how you handle them. Cherish the wins, enjoy them, but understand that the losses will ultimately shape your character. The losses will keep you focused and hungry."

"I don't understand. Are you saying that losing is better than winning?"

"Absolutely not. Winning *is* better. That's why we compete. It's just that even the best will lose more than they win, so you have to learn how to handle the losses.

Remember, even the best hitters in baseball lose seven out of ten times. Cherish the hits, but learn from the outs. And another thing…remember that win or lose, when you walk with God, you never lose. You always win. Don't ever forget that. You always score the winning touchdown with him and you will never be denied a win."

"Well, I understand that, Dad. I do. But I still want to win the game."

"You should, and I hope you do. But just so you know, I'm proud of you and I love you either way."

"I love you too, Dad."

It began to drizzle and we headed out of the park.

# CHAPTER 24

## DECEMBER 17, 1977
## THE CHAMPIONSHIP

UNDER A GRAY DECEMBER SKY, AND WITH THE TEMPERA-
ture in the mid-thirties, we arrived at the field at 1:00 p.m.,
shocked to see how bad it looked. It had rained throughout
the night and into early morning. The snow from a few days
earlier had been replaced with mud. Simply put, the field
was a mess. We walked around the field, hoping that we
would start feeling better about the situation, but could only
exchange worried glances.

"Well, at least we don't have to shovel it," Andy said, trying
to be funny.

Tommy turned to survey the entire field. "I don't know …"

John did his own assessment, and then addressed the
group. "We definitely can't run the usual offense. We've got
to run inside and keep the passes quick."

"Look, it's the same for both teams," I said, trying to find something positive to say. "Let them worry about it. We should just play."

"Yeah, let's just play," said Steve. "The field has nothing to do with the game."

*"I hope he's right."* I thought to myself and began my warm up.

John and I met the other captains at midfield for the coin toss. I looked directly at Bobby.

"Told you we'd be here."

"Never doubted it," Bobby answered, a hint of a smile forming on his face.

John, holding a coin between two fingers, stepped up to Bobby, looked him in the eye, and said, "You're the champs—well, at least for the next 60 minutes—so it's your call: heads or tails."

John's statement hung in the air for a few seconds before Bobby smiled at him. He was not intimidated by what John had said, and like all great athletes, he believed that his team would win. He continued to smile at John. I had seen that smile before. It meant that Bobby was confident and ready.

"We'll take heads," he finally answered.

John flipped the coin. It fell to the ground and landed on tails, but I gave Bobby the ball anyway. Although he tried not to show it (he hesitated for the briefest moment), I could tell he was slightly surprised. I knew that John was surprised as well, but to his credit, he said nothing. John and Bobby quickly exchanged handshakes and wished each other good luck. Bobby and I then shook hands firmly and leaned into each other, almost hugging. As we pulled back, our eyes met and for a moment I felt close to him, knowing that we were both chasing the same dream. The feeling quickly passed and I checked him over for any sign of weakness. There was none.

It was time to play.

John and I began to walk back to our team, but before we got to them, he asked, "Why'd you give them the ball?"

"Field position. It's going to be important today."

"Okay," John nodded, understanding. "Now all we have to do is stop them."

"No problem," I said, confidently.

Both teams huddled for last minute instructions.

"This is it," John said loudly. "One more time boys...let's make it count. Okay, on three...one, two, and three ..."

We all joined in, in perfect unison, "Nothing more! Nothing less! Nothing more! Nothing less!"

We lined up and kicked off to St. Charles. The ball was returned to the St. Charles 20-yard line. As the teams lined up, we surprised St. Charles with an eight-man line. The ball was hiked and pitched to Ross on a sweep left. He was quickly cut off from the outside. He tried to cut in and was met by the interior linemen. No gain.

Second down was also a sweep, this time to the right. Same result. No gain. On third down, an attempted screen pass was batted away. St. Charles was forced to punt the ball.

The kick came off the side of the punter's foot, rolling out of bounds, and we took over the ball at the St. Charles 40-yard line. We struck quickly with three solid running plays, but the drive stalled at the 15-yard line. We set up for the field goal. As I settled into my position of holder, Steve lined himself up for the kick and I felt his hand on my shoulder.

"Which way is the wind blowing?" he asked nervously.

"There is no wind," I answered, trying to calm his nerves. "Just kick it straight."

The snap was on target, and as I placed the ball down, I could feel the ground shake. Steve ran towards the ball and made contact with it. The ball left my hand and the kick felt solid. I closed my eyes briefly, and then opened them to see the ball fly right through the middle of the goal post. The kick was good.

Holy Child-3

St. Charles-0

The game resumed and the teams continued to trade possessions. Neither team was able to move the ball effectively, but our strategy to stop Ross was working. We did not allow him to get outside for any significant gains, and had established control of the middle of the field.

With a minute to go in the half, St. Charles had the ball at midfield. On third down, the quarterback faked a handoff to Ross, who ran into the line. Our linebacker lost sight of him for a moment in the confusion of bodies. The quarterback looked to his right and the linebacker followed him. Ross emerged from the left side of the line. The linebacker spotted him a moment too late, and Ross ran past him. The quarterback lobbed a perfect pass over the linebacker's head. Ross caught the ball in full stride. The other defenders tried to reverse their field and catch Ross. It was too late. He was gone, crossing the end-zone line to the cheers of the St. Charles team. The extra point was good.

St. Charles-7

Holy Child-3

The half ended a few plays later.

We sat in the end zone in silence, oblivious to the mud and cold.

Steve broke the silence, "Can you believe that!" he said in annoyance. We held the son-of-a-gun for the whole half, and with a minute to go, he scores."

"It's okay," Tommy said to the team. "The defense is working. That was all they got the first half."

I sensed that the timing of the touchdown late in the half had taken a toll on the team. I tried to encourage everyone. "Tommy's right. Keep playing the same way and we'll be okay. We're getting the ball to start the half; let's make sure we start the right way."

As I moved back onto the field for the second half, John grabbed my arm. He looked me in the eye, with a hint of sadness in his, and said, "Can you believe it's almost over? We've been waiting for this game since we were ten years old ... and now there's only thirty minutes left."

I understood what he meant. It seemed that all the moments we were so looking forward to were quickly passing by. As he walked away, I smiled to myself. He always saw the big picture in all things—he had ever since we were little kids. I marveled at the way he always seemed to take everything in, and could recall details that almost everyone else had forgotten.

I was lost in that thought when the referee blew the whistle. My thoughts quickly turned back to the game. Both teams lined up for the kick-off. As he approached the ball, the St. Charles kicker slipped and kicked a low line drive. The ball bounced off an unsuspecting Holy Child player and both teams raced for it. The pile unfolded with a St. Charles player in possession of the ball.

St. Charles now had the ball on our 40-yard line. On first down, the ball was faked to Ross on a sweep. Our defense, once again keying on Ross, froze for a split second, which allowed the receiver to get a stride on our safety. The quarterback lofted a perfect bomb to the receiver, who strolled into the end zone untouched. The extra point was good.

St. Charles-14

Holy Child-3

As we walked out of the end zone, I looked at John. He looked away from me and for the first time today, fear and doubt crept into my mind. Maybe it wasn't meant to be. I never really considered that we would lose.

The game moved on. Our defense continued to keep Ross and their offense in check, but our offense could not move the ball on the muddy field against the tough St. Charles defense.

Only five minutes remained when we took over the ball on our own 40-yard line. John called the huddle to attention and called out the play. No one looked at him, because all heads were hung low...and no one said a word. John sensed what we were all feeling, though. We were beaten. The fight was gone. It was over. He stepped back from the huddle, shocked that we would not put up a fight. Silence hung in the air for a few seconds, and then John suddenly stepped back in and shouted, "Everybody look at me!

"You guys are acting like this is over! We got five minutes left to live here."

There was no response. No one, including myself, acknowledged his plea. Our heads continued to hang low. He was alone and he knew it. So he braced himself, pulled his shoulders back, and raised his head slightly. "You know what? Be that way! I'll do it myself!" he said defiantly. "Quarterback option right on one!" As he walked away, he shouted at us, "Block someone!" We approached the line of scrimmage.

Standing behind the center, he looked over the defense and then barked the signals. "Ready, set, hut one!" Running right, he was instantly hit by a vicious shot to the chest. Unwilling to concede, he stumbled ahead and was tackled violently after a three-yard gain. He walked back to the huddle slowly. He looked at no one, calling the same play. Once again, he was tackled hard, but this time gained four yards.

Third down and three yards to go.

"Same play," he said, but did not enter the huddle. He ran again. Four yards and a first down, but the tackle was even harder than the previous two. John picked himself off the ground slowly, and walked painfully back to the huddle. When he tried to call the next play, the air left his lungs and he couldn't speak. He bent over to relieve the pain.

I walked over to him and put my hand on his back. With my hand there, I looked around the huddle and knew what I had to do. I made a fist with my other hand, put it in the middle of the huddle and whispered, "Nothing more! Nothing less!"

One by one, each player extended his fist into the middle of the huddle.

I looked at John confidently.

"Call the play."

We broke the huddle with a purpose. We ran five plays that gained thirty-five yards. We could feel the St. Charles defense starting to bend under the strain of our inspired play. The ball was on the St. Charles 35-yard line with one minute and forty-five seconds remaining in the game. As I jogged back to the huddle, John was waiting for me.

"We need a quick one. Can you take him?" he asked.

"Yeah," I responded, trying to catch my breath.

"Post or flag?"

"Flag," I said confidently. "But give me a chance to set him up inside."

"Maximum protection. I need time." John turned back to the huddle.

The huddle broke. As he approached the center, John purposely never looked to my side of the field. He motioned to the other receiver on the left side. Starting to call the signals, he noticed the safety slowly moving to his right to cover the left receiver. The fake had worked. John knew that I would have single coverage. At the snap of the ball, John immediately looked left, while I ran straight down the field. After fifteen yards, I made a hard cut inside. The cornerback covering me was forced to turn his back to me to cover the inside route. As he turned, I immediately cut back to the outside of the field and headed for the end zone flag. Seeing my second cut, John lofted the ball towards the flag. The ball and I arrived at the same time.

Touchdown!

And the extra point was good.

St. Charles-14

Holy Child-10

As the rest of us celebrated, John dashed over to the two timekeepers and frantically asked, "How much time? How much time?"

"One minute, thirty-one seconds."

"We have all three time outs, right?"

"Yeah, all three."

We huddled before the kick-off.

"You have to kick it high and deep," Tommy said, as he handed the ball to Andy. "We need time to get there."

"Got it!" Andy nodded.

Just before the huddle broke, John called out, "Gotta go all out guys. Stop 'em now...and then three and out."

Andy kicked off. The kick was high and deep, just like we needed. The ball came down on the 20-yard line, and the runner was quickly tackled by several players. As we lined up, John once again asked the timekeepers, "How much time?"

"One minute, twenty-one seconds."

"I got the timeouts!" John shouted, ensuring that the timekeepers would keep him in their sights.

On first down, St. Charles ran a sweep to the right for a gain of two yards. John jumped up, calling for a time out.

"Time out Holy Child!" the timekeeper yelled. "One minute and fourteen seconds left!"

On second down, St. Charles tried a quarterback sneak. The play gained only three yards.

John called time out again and the timekeeper shouted, "Time out Holy Child! One minute and eight seconds! Holy Child only has one time out left!"

It was now third down with five yards to go for a first down. We knew that if St. Charles got a first down, all they would have to do is run out the clock. We had to stop them to have any chance to win the game. We lined up for the crucial third-down play. The ball was snapped to the quarterback, who faked a handoff to Ross, trying to cross up our defense with a pass. The fake was executed perfectly, as the halfback slipped out to the right side. The quarterback lofted a perfect pass that touched the St. Charles' player's hands just as John hit him with a devastating tackle. This knocked the ball up in the air before it fell to the ground. We were still alive. The clock stopped with one minute to go.

We lined all eleven players up at the line of scrimmage, hoping to block the punt, but the ball was punted away by the St. Charles kicker. The ball hit the ground at the Holy Child 40-yard line and stopped at the 30-yard line. As we took over, there were only fifty-eight seconds left.

I walked to the huddle, thinking of what John had said at halftime. It was almost over. One minute left. Win or lose, I didn't want it to end. I watched as my friends entered the huddle. I loved these guys and knew that every moment that passed would be one less we had to spend together. My focus returned to the game when John called the huddle to order: "Let's go guys! Sprint right option on one."

On first down, the ball was snapped to John. Rolling to his right, he started to run but the St. Charles linebacker stepped up to confront him. He saw me break free and threw over the linebacker toward the right sideline. I caught the ball and stepped out of bounds, stopping the clock. The play gained twelve yards.

"Fifty-one seconds!" the timekeeper shouted to John, "Fifty-one seconds!" Back in the huddle, John calmly addressed the team. "Keep working the sideline. Make sure you get out of bounds. Sprint left option on two."

The same play was run to the left side. The play took a little longer to develop this time, as John had to avoid an 'on rushing' defender. The pass was completed to Andy on the left sideline as he quickly stepped out of bounds. The play gained seventeen yards. John looked to the timekeeper.

"Forty seconds!"

John entered the huddle and his eyes searched for me. He gave me *that* look. In all the years we had known each other, I hadn't seen that look often...but I knew what it meant: "Help me."

"They'll overplay the sideline now," I said, and looked around the huddle. "Let's go up the middle with a pass. We still have a time out left."

John thought for a moment and then looked at Tommy. "Tommy, line up tight right and run directly up the seam.

After twenty yards, look back at me. I'm gonna drill it, so be ready."

Tommy nodded.

"One more thing," John added. "I don't want to use the timeout yet. If we complete the pass, everyone hustle down field and line up, and I'll spike the ball to stop the clock."

As we lined up, I noticed that both safeties were lined up wide. "This play could break for a touchdown," I thought to myself. At the snap, John looked to his right, and then quickly snapped his head back to Tommy, who was running down the middle of the field. He fired a hard pass. Tommy caught the ball on the 25-yard line and was tackled immediately. Each player ran up to the ball and set himself. John grabbed the ball, quickly shouted, "Hut!" and spiked the ball. We all turned to the timekeeper.

"Twenty-five seconds!"

John gave a quick look at the St. Charles defense before bending down into the huddle.

"Okay, we probably have time for three plays. Work the outside and the middle and get open."

The ball was snapped to John. As he started back, our center stepped on John's foot, causing him to stumble backwards. He regained his balance but couldn't see above the line. He turned to his left as a defender approached, then started to run right, looking down field. I was all alone in the end zone, waving my arms. He saw me and planted his feet to fire the pass to me, but before he could let go, he was hit hard from behind and landed violently on his stomach. Rolling over, he looked at the timekeeper. "Time out! Time out!" he yelled, barely able to get the words out.

The timekeeper looked at the clock and shouted, "Time out! Time out! Ten seconds to play. No more timeouts."

The play lost fifteen yards. The ball was now on the 40-yard line with no timeouts. We huddled up for one last time. John turned to me. "What do you think?"

"We only have time for one more play," I said, hoping he would understand.

"You think it will work?" he questioned.

"It could," I said, not sounding very confident.

John turned back to the huddle. "Listen up. We're gonna run the play we practiced yesterday. Does everyone remember what to do?" There was some hesitation and murmuring, followed by nods of understanding. John looked around for Tommy in the huddle. "Tommy, make sure you delay long enough or you'll give it away. On two, on two."

The huddle broke and we scrambled to take our positions. "Hey!" John called out. We turned to look at him and then smiled at each other, because at that moment, we knew that these were the greatest friends we would ever have.

"Hey!" John called out again, and then continued, speaking calmly and quietly: "Nothing more! Nothing less!"

"Nothing more! Nothing less!" We fiercely yelled back.

As we approached the line, I could hear Bobby shouting to his teammates. "Back up! They have to go in. They only have time for one play. Everyone get back!" Listening to their captain, six of the defensive players backed up between the 5-yard line and the end zone.

John barked out our signals. I was wide to the right; Tommy was in the back field.

"Hut one! Hut two!"

John took the snap, backpedaling quickly. I sprinted down the middle of the field. Tommy delayed for a few seconds, and then ran the same route that I did...only slightly to the right. John looked to his left to freeze the defense for a moment. I stopped at the 20-yard line, turning to face John. He threw the ball to me. As soon as the ball was let go, I could hear Bobby screaming to his defense: "Ball! Ball! It's short! Get Parisi!"

The ball floated in the air for what seemed like forever. I could hear the defenders charging at me from behind. At the same time, Tommy was racing down the right sideline. As the ball arrived in my hands, I could see Tommy out of the corner of my left eye, about five feet behind me. I tossed the ball to him just as Ross and two other defenders crashed into me. "You didn't get it Parisi!" Bobby shouted as he lay on top of me.

I rolled over and held out my empty hands. "No ball, Ross."

Bobby swiftly turned his head to see Tommy running down the sideline. There were no defenders near him. He crossed the goal line as the clock hit 0.00.

Final Score:

Holy Child-16

St. Charles-14

Our team broke into a mad and frenzied celebration and ran to the end zone to congratulate Tommy. As I hit the end zone, John hugged me and then lifted me up. "*YOU* did it! You son-of-a-gun! *YOU* called it! I can't believe it!"

"Oh yeah! Oh we did it! We did it!" I said, as I lifted my arms upward and savored the moment of victory.

Afterwards, we walked out to the 20-yard line where the St. Charles team was lined up. All players walked through the line, offering congratulations and condolences. Bobby and I were the last people in our lines. When we faced each other, he forced a tired and dejected smile.

"Congratulations. You guys deserved it."

Seeing the pain in his face, I tried to be as compassionate as possible. "Hey, any day it could have been you."

"Yeah, but not today," he said sadly.

"No, not today."

We hugged, tapped each other on the head, and walked away. "Hey! Parisi!" Bobby called out and I turned around. "Where'd you get that play?"

"My dad," I answered.

A knowing smile crossed his face. He knew, as I did, that many of the best plays in a young man's life come from his father.

I smiled back at him, then turned away to join the celebration.

Tommy had a camera. He handed it to the scorekeeper and asked him to take a photo of the team. "Hey! Hey, Guys! Team photo!" he yelled to get everyone's attention.

Suddenly, memories of all the things my friends and I had done over the years began racing through my mind. I thought about the pool parties, the snowball fights, the forts we built, the games we had played, and all the great times we'd had together. It was all here. It was all captured right here. We were complete.

We gathered around slowly. We were muddy, wet, and tired. The hair on our heads hung like damp mops and our bones ached. But it didn't matter. We felt great. Some of us knelt, some of us sat, and some of us stood with our arms around each other's shoulders. The picture was taken.

I still have it.

It sits in a frame on the desk in my office, and every time I look at it, I'm reminded of why it was so special. There were no medals. No trophies. No newspaper articles. No parents telling us how wonderful we were. Just the simple knowledge that, for one day, we were the best. We celebrated for our-selves, for our innocence, and for our friendship.

Nothing more. Nothing less.

# Chapter 25

# December 22, 1977

It was Thursday and school had just let out for the Christmas holiday. I walked down to the main street and caught the bus to the Staten Island Mall. I was going to buy Lauren a Christmas gift. I was nervous. What should I get her? What if she didn't like it? What if she thought it was stupid? I had never bought a gift for a girl before. This pressure was worse than the football game.

I walked around the mall for a while, not really looking for anything in particular, just hoping that something would catch my eye. Before long, I found myself at Macy's jewelry counter. All girls liked jewelry right? Looking at the display cases, I walked back and forth and grew even more nervous when I realized that most of the items were too expensive for me. I had saved about $50 from working my paper route and shoveling snow and I hoped that it would be enough.

The sales woman behind the counter must have seen the worry on my face and quickly came over. "Can I help you honey?" she said, sweetly.

"Um, I'm not sure."

"Are you looking for something in particular?"

"Uh, not really."

"Well, is it for someone special?"

"Yes it is," I said, hoping she wouldn't ask who it was for.

She smiled and sensing my discomfort, she leaned forward and whispered, "Is it for a young lady?"

"It is," I whispered back.

"Okay honey, come with me."

She led me to the other side of the counter, opened the display case, took out a thin gold necklace with a pearl on the end, and handed it to me. It was very pretty.

"How much is it?" I asked, worried that it might be too much.

She turned the tag over, "It's thirty dollars."

I could get it!!! I was so excited!

"I'll take it."

"She'll love it. I can wrap this for you if you'd like."

"Thank you, but I thought I would wrap it myself. Could I just have the wrapping paper?"

"Okay, I'll cut a piece for you to take home." She showed me several types of wrapping paper and I chose a red one with tiny white snowflakes on it. I thought Lauren would like it.

I left Macy's happy and began my trek out of the mall. *"I think she'll really like it,"* I thought to myself, *"It's a nice gift."* But a moment later my nervousness returned. *"What if she doesn't like it? What if she thinks it's stupid? What if it's not enough?"* My thoughts rambled. I opened the box and looked at the necklace. It was really very pretty and the sales lady said that she would love it. *"Yes,"* I thought, *"Lauren will love it."* My doubts disappeared.

I found myself in front of the 'Record Factory' and walked in. The front display rack held the 'Top Albums of 1977'. I noticed that the new Fleetwood Mac album, *Rumours,* was on the rack, and I remembered that Lauren really liked Fleetwood Mac. This was great! I had just enough money left over to also buy her the album. I knew it would make her happy.

I left the mall excited. I had bought my first presents for a girl...and not just any girl. The girl was my girlfriend. The girl was Lauren. We were going to exchange gifts the following day at her house. I couldn't wait.

Lauren and I sat in her living room. Her parents had left us alone to watch TV and exchange our gifts. "You first," I said, and handed her the two gifts.

"Let's take turns," she said, and gave me three gifts. "I want you to go first."

I reached for a long, cylindrical gift and started to unwrap it.

"I hope you like it."

"I'm sure I will."

It was a poster of Ace Frehley, from KISS, playing his famous smoking guitar. The poster had just hit the stores and Lauren knew that Ace was my favorite band member. "This is so cool!" I said excitedly, when I finished uncurling it.

"I'm so glad you like it," she said.

"It's really cool. I was going to buy it for myself. Thank you. Okay, now you," I said, and pointed to the album.

Clearly she knew what it was by its shape, but nevertheless asked "I wonder what this could be?" She ripped the paper quickly. "Oh My God! The Fleetwood Mac album! This is great! Thank you so much!"

I opened the next two gifts. One was a black T-shirt with a picture of the cover of the KISS 'Destroyer' album on the front, which I immediately pulled on over the shirt I was already wearing. The other was a miniature replica of the Oakland Raiders football helmet. "These are so cool Lauren. Thank you very much! Okay, now you open the last one."

She picked up the small box that I had wrapped myself. "This is very pretty wrapping paper. I really like it." She unwrapped the box slowly and opened it. Her eyes grew wide when she saw the necklace inside. "A pearl...a pearl necklace ... Oh, Michael, this is beautiful!" Lauren took the necklace out and dangled it in front of her, admiring it.

I was relieved. She really liked it.

"I love it. Thank you very much. I'm going to put it on right now!"

She did. Then we hugged and sat together, holding hands and watching TV— me wearing my T-shirt, and Lauren wearing her necklace.

# Chapter 26

## December 24, 1977
## Christmas Eve and "The Ghost to the Post"

It was eleven o'clock, Christmas Eve morning. This Christmas presented a new challenge. The family had decided a few months earlier that it would be nice to spend Christmas Eve as well as Christmas morning together, so that the children could open their presents together. This meant that *all* the gifts needed to be wrapped, packed, and moved to Connie's house without the children noticing.

Dad quietly entered the attic through a drop door that was in Jackie's room. The attic was where he and my mother hid the Christmas gifts for us kids. Every year, soon after Thanksgiving, the stairs leading to the attic would "break". "No one is allowed in the attic. The stairs are broken and it's very dangerous," they would say. Jackie and David were still young so this phenomenon went unquestioned by them.

Mom gathered David and Jackie in her bedroom, which allowed my dad to move freely without the fear of revealing the secret hiding place.

Dad made several trips to the car, his arms crammed with as many gifts as he could carry, while Mom kept Jackie and David occupied in her bedroom. When all the gifts were carefully packed into the trunk, Dad covered them with a blanket.

He re-entered the house and called out to Mom, "All ready, babe."

With this, she sent the kids to wash up and then started down the steps, just as Dad headed up. They met in the middle for a quick kiss and a hug.

"All done?" she asked.

"We're good to go," he whispered. "I just want to wash up quickly and get my wallet. Are the kids ready?"

"Yes. They'll be down in a minute."

Dad leaned in for another kiss then said, "I'll be down in a minute too!" and headed up to their bedroom.

After a quick wash, change of shirt, and a brush of his hair, Dad stood in front of the tall bedroom dresser. He put on his watch, placed his wallet in his back pocket, and then looked around the room to see if he had forgotten anything. While he was looking, Jackie entered the room, a square piece of paper in her hand. "Daddy, you're forgetting the most important part of Christmas morning."

He turned to look at her, only slightly paying attention. "Oh, really, what's that baby?"

She held the paper up. "The prayer Daddy, you forgot the prayer ... the prayer about baby Jesus."

She now had his full attention and he quickly made his way towards her. "How could I forget that? You're right; it is the most important part of Christmas morning."

He knelt down beside her and she handed him the prayer. He pulled her in close and wrapped her in a big hug. "Thank you so much baby," he whispered. "You just saved Christmas."

"You're welcome, Daddy," she answered proudly. "Merry Christmas!" she said, and skipped out of the room singing.

He looked at the prayer, smiled to himself, and put the paper in his back pocket.

When our car pulled up in front of Aunt Connie's house, I could tell that we were probably the last to arrive. The front yard was covered in children—more specifically, my cousins. As we entered the house, my senses were greeted by the smell and sounds of Christmas. Carols floated through the air, as did the fragrance of pine and baking bread. The whole family was together. There were thirteen adults and nineteen children, ranging from three years old to seventeen. While the children drifted in and out of the house, my mother and my aunts found the kitchen, and the men moved into the den.

I looked at the clock. It was 12:20 and the Oakland Raiders were playing the divisional playoff game against the Baltimore Colts, in Baltimore, at 12:30. This was their first playoff game since their victory in Super Bowl XI. Their record of 11-3 placed them second to the Denver Broncos, making them the AFC Wild-Card team. The Colts were a good team, a solid team, but they weren't the Steelers, the Chiefs, or the Broncos—all traditional rivals. My father, uncles, and I viewed the Colts as nothing more than a formality on the road to the Super Bowl.

Man, were we wrong! What happened on December 24th, 1977 would become part of NFL history.

As the pre-game ended, we gathered around the television. "Let's go Raiders!" Uncle Tom shouted and clapped his hands.

"Who are these Colts? The Colts? No problem," Uncle Paul chimed in.

The teams engaged in a tight defensive struggle until midway through the first quarter.

On first down from the Colt 30-yard line, Ken Stabler handed off to Clarence Davis, who burst through a huge hole on the left side. Davis faked out a defender, and then pushed off safety Lyle Blackwood at the 5-yard line for a touchdown.

We jumped up, cheering the score. "All right! Way to go!" Dad roared.

"It was just a matter of time!" Uncle Tom added exuberantly. We exchanged handshakes.

Errol Mann kicked the extra point and the Raiders took the lead by seven.

Early in the second quarter, the Raiders had the ball on the Colt 48-yard line.

On third down, Stabler dropped back, looked left, then turned to throw right to Van Eeghan on the right sideline. Colts cornerback Bruce Laird stepped in front of Van Eeghan at the Colt 40-yard line, intercepted the ball, and returned it sixty yards for a Colts touchdown.

"Oh no!" Uncle Paul yelled, as he turned to the others.

Dad slumped back into his chair as he looked at Rich.

"Gave them a gift...can't do that in this kind of game."

Tony Linhart kicked the extra point:

Raiders-7

Colts-7

The defensive battle continued. Late in the quarter, the Colts marched from their 20-yard line to the Raider 20-yard line. The defense stiffened and the Colts settled for a field goal. The first half ended.

Colts-10

Raiders-7

Everyone who watched the game glumly headed to the kitchen to mingle with the others, and to eat some Christmas Eve dinner specialties before the second half began. Dinner on Christmas Eve was always a feast of delights from the ocean, and this always managed to lift everyone's spirits— even when your team was not doing so well in their game. The table was literally covered with seafood. There were dozens of baked clams on three long trays, two bowls of cold octopus salad, several bowls of fried calamari, and several huge bowls of fried jumbo shrimp. As I said, a feast!

I made myself a plate and sat down to eat. Mom went over to where Dad was sitting, and asked, "How's the game going?"

"Not good," he mumbled, staring into his plate.

"Really?" Aunt Connie said, surprised. Then she added, almost arrogantly, "The Raiders can't lose to the Colts!"

"They won't; they won't," Uncle Rich quickly interjected.

"They better not," Uncle Tom said, to no one in particular.

"They'll be okay; it's early yet," Uncle Paul added, as he reached for more food.

"I hope so," Aunt Connie said, heading back to the stove to cook more delights from the deep blue sea.

I finished eating, and was about to head back to the TV for the second half of the game, when I looked up and saw Uncle Rich sneak up behind Aunt Connie and give her a hug. "Connie, that was simply delicious."

She turned and kissed him on the cheek. "Thanks! Love you," she said, affectionately.

"Love you too," he replied, as he ran back to the den to watch the game. It was good to see these family members appreciate each other and not be afraid to show it.

And the game called us back ...

As we settled back into our seats, the sense of anticipation, mingled with deep concern, was thick in the air. For a brief moment, I thought, *"Could we lose to the Colts?"* That thought quickly disappeared as soon as the game started.

The Raiders kicked off to start the third quarter. Three plays and out for the Colts and the Raiders took over at their 30-yard line.

Uncle Rich looked at Dad. "We needed that stop."

"Yes, we did." Dad agreed.

The ball belonged to the Raiders. On second down, Ken Stabler faded back, looked around, and then threw deep down the left sideline. Cliff Branch made a leaping catch over Colt defender Lloyd Munsey at the Colt 30-yard line. On third down, Stabler dropped back to pass. As Colt defender John Dutton grabbed at his ankle, he stepped up and passed to Dave Casper, who caught the pass just as he crossed the goal line.

TOUCHDOWN!

The room jumped to life.

Mann kicked the extra point.

Raiders-14

Colts-10

The game was interrupted by a commercial break.

Dad looked around the room and said to everyone, "Okay, they should be all right now."

"Yep, you're right," Uncle Tom agreed. "The Colts will fold now."

As the words left Uncle Tom's mouth, the game came back on the television and Ray Guy kicked off for the Raiders. The ball was received by Marshall Johnson on the 13-yard line. Johnson started straight and then veered to his left. A huge hole opened, and Marshall ran through. No one on the Raiders touched him. He went eighty-seven yards.

TOUCHDOWN!

"I don't believe it. Can you believe this?" Uncle Rich said frantically as he jumped out of his seat.

Dad didn't respond, his face buried in his hands.

Linhart kicked the extra point.

Colts-17

Raiders-14

"Ahh, we'll be all right," Uncle Tom said. "We'll be all right." No one answered. Now we weren't so sure.

The teams traded possessions and the Colts prepared to punt the ball. As the ball was snapped, linebacker Ted Hendricks slid past the blocker in front of him, blocking the punt. The bouncing ball was recovered by Jeff Barnes who returned the ball to the Colt 16-yard line.

"Oh Yeah!" Uncle Paul screamed. Dad looked right at me. "We needed that. Can't waste it now. We gotta get a touchdown."

Uncle Rich agreed. "You're right; a field goal doesn't help us here."

The Raiders took over.

On first down, Stabler handed to Van Eeghan, who went four yards up the middle. On second and six, Stabler again handed to Van Eeghan, who gained two yards. On third down, Stabler faded back to pass. He looked left, before turning to the middle and finding Casper alone on the goal line. Casper made the catch and turned into the end zone.

TOUCHDOWN!

Dad jumped up. "Yes! Yes! Yes!"

"C'mon now, end this nonsense," Uncle Rich said, expressing his exasperation.

Mann kicked the extra point.

Raiders-21

Colts-17

That ended the third quarter.

As the fourth quarter began, the Colts started a drive on their 20-yard line.

On first down, Jones went back to pass. He threw right, completing a pass to Glen Doughty at the 40-yard line. Two incomplete passes made it third and ten. Jones faded back and completed a pass to Mitchell, over the middle, for twenty-two yards to the Raider 38-yard line. Two successful running plays and the Colts advanced to the Raider 1-yard line. First and goal at the 1-yard line.

"This is a key moment!" Uncle Paul shouted. Of course, no one answered him—we were all glued to the screen.

On first down, Jones handed off to Lee up the middle. No gain.

On second down, Jones handed off to Lee to the left side. No gain.

On third down, Jones handed off to McCauley, who dove for the end zone but was met violently by Raider linebacker Monte Johnson. The violent hit left Johnson on the field in pain, kicking his legs and awaiting medical attention. As we watched him walk off the field, Dad looked around the room and said, "We stop them here and they'll quit."

Uncle Tom pleaded with the television screen: "Come on, one stop! One time!"

The teams lined up. Jones took the snap, turned, and handed the ball to Lee. He leaned to the middle, leaping and crossing the goal line (just barely).

**TOUCHDOWN!**

"C'mon!" Uncle Tom waved dejectedly.

Uncle Paul bowed his head and then looked up. "I can't take much more of this."

Linhart made the extra point.

Colts-24

Raiders- 21

10:28 left in the game.

Linhart kicked off. The ball was received by Garret at the 4-yard line. He ran left, returning the ball to the Raider 47-yard line.

"Excellent! Great field position," Dad growled, as he paced the floor.

On third and ten, Stabler dropped back, dumping off a seven-yard pass to Van Eeghan, who faked a linebacker and rumbled to the Colt 29-yard line for a twenty-four-yard completion.

Uncle Tom's whole focus was locked on the TV screen. "We're moving now."

On first down, Stabler faded back to pass, looked right, then passed long to the left side of the end zone, where Branch waited. Munsey ran into Branch. A penalty was called on the Colts, resulting in a first and goal for the Raiders on the Colt 1-yard line.

"All right. Put it in now!" Dad shouted.

On first and goal, Stabler turned and handed the ball to Pete Banazak, who dove over the right side for a touchdown.

"Awwwright!!" We all shouted together.

Mann kicked the extra point.

**Raiders-28**

**Colts-24**

During the commercial we sat back, trying to catch our breath and calm ourselves.

Uncle Rich leaned forward laughing. "This is unbelievable."

"I'm not gonna make it," Uncle Paul said. He literally looked exhausted.

"I think we'll be okay now," Uncle Tom added, rising from the couch again.

The game returned. Ray Guy kicked off for the Raiders. The ball was received by Johnson at the 2, and he returned it to the Colt 27-yard line.

Jones dropped back, passing the ball to Raymond Chester down the middle of the field. Chester was immediately hit hard by Skip Thomas but held onto the ball, resulting in a thirty-yard completion. On the next play, Jones flipped a screen pass to Lee, who took the ball down to the Raider 28-yard line. Jones then handed the ball to Lee, who swept left for a thirteen-yard gain down to the Raider 15-yard line. Once again, Jones handed to Lee, who burst through the middle, running fifteen yards for a touchdown.

Four plays—73 yards and a touchdown!

The room grew silent again.

*"Maybe this is the end."*

*"Maybe the Raiders don't have anything left."*

*"Maybe it's over."*

Linhart kicked the point.

Colts-31

Raiders-28

The Raiders and Colts did not move the ball on the next two possessions. The Raiders got the ball back with 2:55 left in the game and the ball on their 30-yard line.

The game stopped for a commercial break.

I got up from my seat and sat down next to Dad. He put his arm around me and looked around the room.

"I don't know guys. Not looking good."

Uncle Rich waved him off. "You're crazy. Guaranteed Stabler gets us in."

"Hope so," Dad whispered, and turned back to the TV.

The game came back on. On first down, Stabler threw right to Davis, who caught the ball and was tackled at the 44-yard line. First down. The next play was an incomplete pass. On second and ten, Stabler went back to pass, looked left, pump faked, then threw deep to the right side. The pass was intended for Casper but was over thrown. Casper (with his back to Stabler) turned to his right, looking over his shoulder. As he looked, the ball dropped straight over his head into his outstretched hands—an amazing pass and catch that took the ball down to the Colt 14-yard line.

"Oh my God, did you see that!?" Uncle Tom shouted, pointing to the screen.

"What a catch! What a catch! What a catch!" Uncle Rich kept screaming.

The NBC game crew was also amazed at the catch. They showed it from several different angles. The announcer stated that "Dave Casper looked as if he just popped out of the grass and appeared the moment the ball arrived."

"Greatest catch I've ever seen," Dad added.

Uncle Paul did not move from his chair. "I can't take much more of this."

What none of us knew at the time was the origin of the play. During the fourth quarter, Raider assistant coach Tom Flores noticed that the Colt safeties were sneaking in

towards the line of scrimmage. He sent in running back
Mark Van Eeghan and told him to "tell Stabler to look for
Ghost to the post."

Tight end Dave Casper's nickname was Ghost, and he
wanted him to run a post pattern. Ghost to the Post, get it?

The Raiders resumed the drive, and on fourth down,
attempted a field goal.

It was good.

Raiders-31

Colts-31

After 60 minutes, nothing had been settled and the game
moved to overtime.

Captains for both teams met with the officials for the coin
toss to determine which team would have possession first.

Neither team could move the ball on their first few possessions. The Raiders then took over and went forty-one
yards in nine plays, setting up for the winning field goal.

We leaned in closer to the TV. "C'mon put it through,"
Uncle Rich begged.

The teams lined up. The ball was snapped; Mann kicked
the ball. It was blocked and the Colts took over.

"No! No!" We yelled.

Uncle Paul still hadn't moved. "I *really* can't take much
more of this."

Late in the first overtime, the Raiders took over again, and
on third down and nineteen, Stabler faded back, passing the
ball to Branch, who made a diving catch at the 26-yard line.

First down!

Two plays netted another first down as the first overtime period ended. The teams changed sides.

On first down, Stabler handed to Banazak for a 2-yard gain. Now that they were easily in field goal range, the Colts expected the Raider offense to run the ball. Sensing this, Stabler crossed up the Colt defense by lofting a perfect pass to Casper in the left corner of the end zone.

TOUCHDOWN!

The room erupted. The sounds of victory (and maybe some relief too) filled the air. Dad and Uncle Rich hugged in celebration and then they both hugged me. Uncle Tom hugged and "danced" with his son, while Uncle Paul slowly rose from the couch, looking as though he would pass out at any moment from all the excitement.

The Raiders won.

Final Score:

**Raiders-37**

**Colts-31**

It was over, and the Raiders won. What we all thought of as a formality had become an epic struggle for survival. The Raiders had once again demonstrated their commitment to excellence and had given Raider fans and NFL fans another great memory.

The game had everything in it. For the record, the game was played for 76 minutes—the third longest game in

NFL history. There were 68 points scored, 9 lead changes, a blocked punt, a blocked field goal, a kickoff return for a touchdown, an interception for a touchdown, and one broken neck.

Yes, Raider linebacker Monte Johnson had in fact broken a bone in his neck. Unaware of the extent of his injury, he returned to the game and led the Raiders with a career high of 20 tackles.

# CHAPTER 27

# PERFECT

EVENTUALLY EVERYONE SETTLED DOWN FROM THE excitement of the game. The children, now indoors, ran around playing various games of their own. Dad, Uncle Rich, and Uncle Tom were outside smoking cigars. The other adults were scattered around the house; some sat in the living room relaxing, some watched TV, some were at the dining room table playing cards, and others sat in the kitchen picking at leftovers.

Uncle Jim was sitting on the sofa, relaxing, when my sister Jackie went up to him and asked, "Uncle Jim, can you play the guitar so we can sing Christmas carols?"

He paused for moment, trying to remember if his guitar was in his car. "Sure we can sweetie. You go get your cousins and I'll go to my car and get the guitar."

Jackie ran off to get the other children. On his way to the car, Jim remembered that Diana, Connie's oldest daughter, played the piano, so he went looking for her. He found her in the kitchen. "Hey Diana, the kids want to sing some Christmas carols. You up for it?"

"Sure," she replied.

Jim returned with his guitar and joined Diana at the piano. The smaller children had already gathered around her. "Okay, what's first?" she asked, and took out a book, simply titled '*Christmas Carols*,' from the piano bench.

"Rudolph! Rudolph!" shouted Jackie, jumping up and down. The others joined in.

Diana looked at Jim, and he nodded his head slightly. "Okay, Rudolph it is," she said.

Diana started playing the song on the piano, and once Jim picked up the beat, he joined in with his guitar. Diana began singing and the other children soon joined in. They moved onto other Christmas favorites, like '*Jingle Bells*', '*Santa Claus is Coming to Town*,' and '*Frosty the Snowman*,' and as they sang, the adults trickled into the room and began to sing as well. Soon everyone was singing, smiling, and laughing.

"Hey! Hey!" interjected Dad, waving his arms in the air in order to get everyone's attention. "Let's sing '*The Twelve Days of Christmas*'."

"Great idea!" Aunt Connie shouted out, and I immediately thought back to Father Valenti's class and chuckled to myself, feeling extremely smart now that I knew the origins of the song and its ties to Christmas.

The singing and celebration continued around me. I slowly made my way to a corner of the room to watch everyone celebrate. As I watched, I replayed the events of December 1977 in my mind:

I had my first girlfriend, kissed her, and bought her a Christmas present. I saw my favorite rock 'n roll band in concert for the first time. My friends and I had won a championship that could never be taken away from us. I watched the Raiders win an epic game that would go down in NFL history, and most of all, I celebrated a happy and joyous Christmas Eve with my family.

I searched for a word to describe both the events of the month and also my friends, my family, and my life. One word quickly came to mind:

Perfect.

# Chapter 28

# Presents

The clock moved past midnight. It was now December 25, 1977. It was officially Christmas Day. All the small children had been put to bed and were sleeping soundly. Uncle Rich was lying on the couch, and I was sitting with my father and other uncles discussing the game we had watched earlier.

Mom walked in. "The little ones are all sleeping now. We can start. Anthony, we can start now."

At her urging, my father, uncles, and I got up to get the presents from the cars, except for Uncle Rich who was still lying on the couch. My father turned to him. "Rich, are you coming?"

Uncle Rich turned onto his side slowly and stiffly, and quietly asked "Do me a favor. My back is killing me. Can you get the presents from my car?"

"Yeah sure, give me the keys," Dad obliged.

We made several trips back and forth from the car to the house, with armloads of gifts, moving quickly as the cold December night ripped right through us.

Uncle Tom made the last trip in, his arms still crammed with presents.

"Tom, is that it?" asked my mother, as she closed the front door behind him.

"Are you kidding? We took two cars here, one for just the presents!" whined Uncle Tom, but his tone implied amusement.

Of course, Aunt Connie instructed everyone where to place the presents. "Barbara, Tom, bring the gifts here. Let's put them all the way around the tree."

As we were placing the presents around the tree, Uncle Rich let out a small groan. My aunt turned to face him. "You okay?" she asked, a worried look on her face.

"Yeah," he said, groaning again. "My back is really sore."

I walked over to the couch. "You're old!" I teased.

"Not too old to kick your butt," he grinned.

"Anytime Grandpa," I replied, and assumed a fighter's stance.

We laughed. It was a good laugh for both of us.

When all the presents were carefully placed around the tree, Aunt Connie turned down the lights. The Christmas tree lights shone and reflected off the Christmas ornaments and the shiny wrapping paper, ribbons, and bows on the gifts.

"Wow! Will you look at that ..." my father said in admiration.

Silence fell over the room. We all stood by the Christmas tree and admired the beauty of the moment. There were no words but we all felt it. The message was simple: We're all together; we're happy; we're healthy, and we are all blessed to have such a happy and Merry Christmas.

My aunt broke the silence. "How about some coffee?"

# Chapter 29

# How? Why?

It was 2:00 a.m. and I was settled comfortably in a large leather recliner in the living room, watching TV but not really paying attention. Uncle Rich was still lying on the couch and he had begun tossing and softly moaning again.

"Hey Uncle Rich, you okay?" I asked quietly. "Can I get you something?"

He turned to face me, a look of pure anguish on his face. A second later he screamed, and I screamed for my father.

"Dad! Dad! Dad! Hurry!" I kept yelling, not sure of what to do.

My father and some relatives rushed into the room "What? What's going on? What's the matter?" Their anxious voices were strained with worry.

By this time, I was speechless and shaking. I pointed to Uncle Rich, who was clutching his chest and writhing in agony. Dad hurried towards the couch. Just as Uncle Rich started to fall off, Dad knelt down and stopped him. He gently pushed Uncle Rich back onto the couch and quickly examined him to see if he could find any signs of why he was in so much pain.

There were none...because the pain came from inside.

Aunt Connie was the last to come into the living room. "Oh my God!" she screamed, when she spotted Uncle Rich. She ran to the end of the couch, fell to her knees, and gently stroked his head, trying to calm him ... telling him not to worry and that everything would be okay.

"Barbara, call an ambulance! Call 911 now!" Dad yelled out to my mother, all in one breath, and then quietly asked, "Rich, can you hear me?" Uncle Rich didn't answer but I could see that he was awake. The agonized look on his face reflected the pain that his body must have been feeling. The house, which only a moment ago had been calm and peaceful was now frantic with fear. I moved in closer to see him. He looked directly at me, but I could tell that he did not see me. It was if he were looking past me to something beyond that room. His breathing became labored.

Aunt Connie put her lips close to his ear. "I'm here. I'm here, Rich. Don't worry; I'm here with you." She was always there for her brothers. She was there when their father died, and she would not leave Rich now. We all knew it.

Aunt Jeanette gave Aunt Connie a cool cloth and she gently placed it on his forehead. "Hold on Rich; hold on," she quietly implored. Her voice brought him back and he blinked to acknowledge her. But the pain was too great and he cried out once more. There seemed to be no relief from it.

Aunt Connie lifted her head for a moment and met my father's eyes. She looked for assurance. He gave none. His eyes revealed his great fear, and the knowledge that Rich was in trouble. Connie understood and silent tears ran down her face.

After what seemed like an eternity, we finally heard the wail of the ambulance siren. It stopped outside the house, and eerily, its revolving light lit up the entire room. "Thank God, they're here! They're here!" Mom uttered, her voice shaking and barely audible. She rushed to the front door and opened it.

"Help is here Rich," Dad said to comfort him. "Hold on."

Two EMS workers entered the house. The first one headed straight to Uncle Rich, asking "What's his name?" to no one in particular.

"Rich," Aunt Connie answered.

While his partner began probing Uncle Tom for information, the EMS worker looked for visible clues as to what was going on with Rich, quickly realizing that he was having a heart attack. He moved in closer and tried to engage him in some light-hearted conversation. "Hi, Rich. What's going on here? Too much pasta tonight?"

Uncle Rich tried, but could not answer. The second EMS worker began to examine his vital signs.

"BP 90 over 60, Pulse 150, patient is sweating."

The EMS worker tried to get Rich to focus again. "Rich? Rich, can you hear me?"

Uncle Rich finally opened his eyes and nodded faintly.

"Good Rich, good. All right Rich, we gotta take you to the hospital so they can help you. Okay?"

The EMS workers set up the stretcher, gently lifted him onto it, and tied him down. Quiet sobbing took over the room.

"Who's coming in the ambulance?" one of them asked.

Aunt Connie took a step forward, froze for a moment... and then took a step back. She couldn't do it. She couldn't go.

And for the first time in her life, for the first time in all of our lives, she just couldn't be there.

Time was of essence. Dad took over. "I am."

"Okay, let's go."

"Dad?" I called out to him.

When he turned around, I didn't say a word but merely looked at him, as if as if to say, "Can I go too?"

He hesitated for a second, and then motioned to me. "C'mon."

I watched as the stretcher was loaded into the ambulance.

Uncle Tom and Uncle Paul ran for a car. "We'll follow you!" Uncle Tom yelled out to my father.

I got into the ambulance first and sat down quickly. After Dad got in, a hand reached out for his and grabbed it. It was Aunt Connie's. He looked up and their eyes locked.

"Take care of him, Anthony." Her eyes bore into his and her gripped tightened around his hand, even though hers were trembling.

He tried to answer with words, but they did not come out. He answered instead with a quick nod and a blink of his eyes. Their grip was broken as the doors closed.

The ambulance pulled away and Uncle Tom and Uncle Paul followed behind. The ambulance turned the corner and both vehicles disappeared into the night.

At the hospital, the ambulance backed into the emergency room entrance and I could see two doctors waiting as I looked out its window. The doors flew open, the stretcher was quickly removed from the ambulance and wheeled away. Dad and I stepped out of the ambulance. A hospital administrator was waiting to speak with us.

"Are you a family member?"

"Yes, I'm his brother," Dad said, as he looked past her and watched Uncle Rich being wheeled through swinging doors.

"I need some general information. Will you please come with me?"

"Sure, okay ... sure," he answered, not really paying attention.

She led us through the doors and into the waiting room. I sat down on an empty sofa as she led Dad to a small sectioned-off area and began asking questions. Uncle Tom and Uncle Paul joined me on the sofa.

Uncle Tom placed his arm around my shoulders trying to comfort me. "He'll be okay, Michael. He'll be okay," he said, but not very convincingly.

I didn't say anything.

My last words to Uncle Rich just kept going through my mind over and over again: "Any time, Grandpa." I had only spoken those words an hour or so ago, but it seemed like forever...and besides, he wasn't even that old.

My father eventually joined us and we sat in silence. I'm sure we were all reliving the events of the past few hours.

A short while later, a young doctor emerged from the swinging doors. He had a long ponytail that flowed down his back, and as he approached, I noticed that his green scrubs were peppered with red spots of blood.

"One of you is the brother?" he questioned, looking at us.

My father stood up. "Yes. I am."

He hesitated for a moment, rubbed his chin, and stepped closer to Dad. "I'm sorry; there was nothing we could do. He's passed on."

I didn't really understand what was going on, and I looked at my father. He blinked once or twice, but did not say anything. From behind, I felt one of my uncles wrap his arms around me.

My father struggled, "How ... what? What happened?"

The doctor sighed, and then answered, measuring his words carefully. "He had a massive heart attack."

"But he was fine. A few hours ago, he was fine. I don't ..."

"Sometimes there are no warnings," the doctor said, wishing that he had more to give. "I'm very sorry."

As the doctor walked away, my father called out, "Can I see him?"

The doctor hesitated and contemplated Rich's current condition. "Sure," he said quietly. "Give us a few minutes. We tried hard to save him." He walked away, disappearing through the swinging doors.

The four of us sat in shock, trying to make sense of what had just happened.

"Dad, I want to see him too." I had made up my mind.

"No, you shouldn't," Uncle Tom said, wanting to protect me.

My father looked at me gravely. He wanted to be certain that I was ready to handle this.

"I want to see him," I said again, more forcefully.

"Okay," he whispered softly.

A few minutes later, the doctor emerged through the doors. "You can see him now."

We stood up and Dad put his arm around me. We followed the doctor through the swinging doors and into a small gray room. The doctor stood in the doorway as we stepped in. My eyes surveyed the room from right to left. I didn't notice him at first. Then I spotted him. He was on a table near the back wall, with a sheet covering him up to the middle of his chest.

And for the first time in my life I felt real fear.

I did not move forward with my father. Dad reached out for the lifeless hand and I moved to the corner of the room so I could see both of them.

Now it was real.

He was gone.

I had never seen a dead person. I had never seen my dad cry.

That night I saw both.

I watched my father. A single tear ran down his face. Dad bent down towards Uncle Rich and gently stroked the hair away from his face. He placed his right hand on his cheek and kissed his forehead. Dad gazed up to the ceiling for a moment, then buried his head in Uncle Rich's chest. A low wail filled the room. His body shook from his heaving sobs. The look and sound of his crying stunned me completely, and my body jolted as if an invisible force had pushed me backwards.

I had never seen him cry. He was my father. He was always strong. He was always strong for everyone. He was always in control. There was a comfort in that and we all counted on it. My uncle was dead and my father was crying. It was as if I was caught in some awful nightmare.

I'm sure most people can't remember when their childhood really ended. I do. It ended on December 25, 1977. It ended in that room. It ended as I watched my father cry over the body of his dead brother.

As I watched him, I realized that his life and the lives of everyone in our family would never be the same. From somewhere deep inside of me, I knew that the innocence of my youth was gone.

That night I learned that absolutely nothing in life is guaranteed—not even your next breath.

# CHAPTER 30

## NO COMFORT IN THE SILENCE

BACK AT AUNT CONNIE'S HOUSE, MOST OF MY RELATIVES sat around the kitchen table as usual, except that there was nothing usual about this night. Every now and then someone spoke:

"He'll be okay, Connie."

"You'll see; he'll be okay."

"I'm sure everything is gonna be okay, Connie."

"He's gonna be fine; just wait and see."

"It's Christmas, of course he's gonna be fine."

Mom placed a hot cup of coffee in front of Connie. Its aroma wafted through the air and Connie took a deep breath in. But there was no "Aaahhh!" Instead, she stared blankly into the cup and Mom began to gently rub her shoulders.

Eventually, the only sound heard in the kitchen was the sound of silence.

It was 4:30 in the morning when the four of us left the hospital and got into the car, confused and unable to comprehend the events of the last few hours.

We drove home in silence.

Before I knew it, Uncle Tom pulled the car into the driveway and the four of us got out. Dad slowly led the way up the driveway, my uncles and I right behind him. Suddenly, he stopped and turned to us, "How do I tell her? What do I say?" he asked quietly. Desperation clung to his voice.

No one answered. There was only silence.

Even the house was silent and still. No signs of life could be seen or heard from outside.

Dad turned back around, continued up the driveway to the front door, and opened it.

The sound at the door startled everyone, yet no one spoke—silent apprehension thick in the air. Aunt Connie jumped up from her seat and ran to the door. Dad walked through it, surprised to see her standing in front of him. She searched for Rich for a split second, and then looked directly at my father. He looked down. And she knew. Dad stepped forward and reached for her. She knew. Then she fell.

"Oh no! No! No! No, Anthony! No!" she wailed.

The silence was broken.

He knelt down to pick her up off the floor and held her. "I got you Connie; I got you. Don't worry; don't worry. I got you."

She fell forward into his arms. Her head lay against his chest. She cried. She was inconsolable. Dad rocked her back and forth, trying to bring her some measure of comfort—his own silent tears flowing down his face.

And as I glanced around me, I realized that all the adults, who had always comforted me as a child, were now standing together crying. But I could not comfort them and they could not comfort me. They could not even comfort each other.

On this night, there would be no comfort.

The comfort was gone.

The silence was loud.

# Chapter 31

# The Prayer

It was Christmas morning.

I stood at the kitchen counter and sipped a glass of milk. My father and Aunt Connie sat at the kitchen table facing each other. They sat in silence. Dad held Aunt Connie's hand. The rest of my family was either sleeping or quietly scattered around the house.

The stillness of the morning was broken by three of my little cousins, who ran from one of the bedrooms, "Yaaaay! Yaaayy! Santa Claus came! Santa Claus came!"

Aunt Connie and Dad and were startled by the sound of the enthusiastic little voices and both frowned for a moment: Who could be so happy on such a morning? They quickly realized that it was Christmas morning. They had forgotten. Dad got up from the chair. "I'll take care of it," he told Aunt Connie. "I'll tell them to keep it down."

He started to walk away, but she grabbed his arm. "No Anthony. It's Christmas. Let them celebrate. They're just kids."

He smiled at her and then helped her out of her chair. They shared a hug and tried to gather the strength that they would need to get through the morning.

The children, not knowing what had happened, celebrated Christmas morning with the joy and innocence that only children can have, and with the noise that only children can make. After they opened each gift, they enthusiastically shouted out what it was. The opening of the gifts was a lengthy and difficult process for the adults, but to their credit each of them bravely endured it and celebrated along with the children—*for* the children.

Eventually the gift opening came to a close, the children calmed down, and the adults became restrained. A quiet fell over the house.

Jackie walked over to Dad, who stood near the Christmas tree. "It's time, Daddy," she stated purposefully.

He looked down at her, puzzled—not quite understanding.

"The prayer, Daddy," she whispered. "It's time to do the prayer about baby Jesus."

Then it dawned on him. He reached into his back pocket and pulled out the piece of paper she had given him the day before. He looked at it, afraid to open it. He searched for my mother, because he needed assurance from his wife. Her eyes filled with tears and all she could do was nod. Everyone in the room noticed, but did not know what was going on. This was a tradition my father carried out only with us.

He gently unfolded the paper and was momentarily taken aback by the words. He glanced around the room, cleared his throat, and slowly began:

**"And there were in the same country shepherds abiding in the field, keeping watch over their flock by night.**

**And, lo, the angel of the Lord came upon them, and the glory of the Lord shone round about them: and they were sore afraid.**

**And the angel said unto them, fear not: for, behold, I bring you good tidings of great joy, which shall be to all people.**

**For unto you is born this day in the city of David a Savior, which is Christ the Lord.**

**And this shall be a sign unto you; Ye shall find the babe wrapped in swaddling cloths, lying in a manger.**

**And suddenly there was with the angel a multitude of the heavenly host praising God, and saying, Glory to God in the highest and on earth peace, good will toward men."**

No one spoke or moved, except Aunt Connie. She moved into the middle of the room, lowered her head, and very softly said, "Amen".

"Amen," we all replied.

Years later, my father told me that reading the prayer that morning was one of the hardest things he ever had to do in his life.

# CHAPTER 32

# DECEMBER 28, 1977
# THE FUNERAL

ON A BRUTALLY COLD MORNING, LATE IN DECEMBER, the family and friends of Richard Parisi gathered around his casket at Resurrection Cemetery. Large flower arrangements circled the grave site—the hole in the ground covered by a green tarp. Each of us held a red rose. Although it was cold, we could feel the warmth of the sun as it shone on us through a cloudless blue sky.

Father Valenti, his Bible in hand, stood on one side of the casket and faced the mourners, leading them through a series of prayers. When the prayers ended, he sprinkled the casket with Holy Water as he circled around it, and then addressed the crowd.

"Friends, we gather here to celebrate the life of Richard Parisi and his reward for his life on earth. Although we grieve for Richard, we must also rejoice. Rejoice for the fact that he is now with our Father and that no harm will ever come to him again. Rejoice, that through the sacrifice of our savior and Lord Jesus Christ, Richard's life is not over but only beginning.

"For each of you his life meant different things. He was a son, a brother, an uncle, a cousin, and a friend. Because of that, each of you will have special memories of him. Keep those memories close and you will always be close to him. Please join me in prayer for our brother Richard: 'Our father who art in heaven …'"

At the end of the service, I watched friends and family members, young and old, file past the casket. Everyone said goodbye silently, in their own way, and gently dropped their rose on the casket. I walked over to it. It was my first funeral, and I was struck by how small the casket looked—the smallness contrasted with the vastness of life.

Life has a distinct feel, a feeling of freedom, of limitlessness, of being able to open your arms and embrace the world. The casket seemed like such a small and confining place to end your life. There seemed nowhere to go. But then I remembered what Father Valenti said, that this was not the end for Uncle Rich but only a beginning. Although I believed this to be the truth, it somehow offered little comfort.

I dropped my rose and whispered, "I miss you Uncle Rich." I was about to walk away when I noticed my father standing by the casket, tears rolling down his face. With a heavy sigh, he tossed his rose onto the casket and then placed his hand on it, gazing up toward the sky. This was the last goodbye. He was gone and there was nothing that could be done.

Dad wiped the tears from his eyes and we began to slowly walk away. My father and I looked back one more time. Then he put his arm around me and we left the cemetery in silence.

After the funeral, we gathered at Aunt Connie's house. A steady stream of relatives and friends stopped by. Many of them brought large trays of food with them. I sat in the living room, watching and listening. Everything seemed so surreal. My mother and aunts were gathered in the kitchen, attempting to organize all the food that had been so kindly given to us. In the past, whenever I watched my mother and aunts work in there, they were always at ease and in control. Today they were harried, flustered, and out of place. The conversations drifted between topics relating to Uncle Rich and the details of normal everyday life. Everything was odd. My father was quiet and distant, and for the first time in my life I didn't know what to say to him.

Day became night, and before long, everyone had gone ... leaving only my immediate family and Aunt Connie's family together. I looked out the window and realized that a light snow had begun to fall. At one point, Dad got up to talk with his sister. I watched them as they stood a few inches away from each other. I was unable to hear what they were saying. I could only imagine what they were going through. I had a brother and sister and couldn't imagine either of them ever being taken away. I thought about how they had always depended on each other, how they always took care of each other. They were three for so long, and now they were two ... and would forever be incomplete.

On the way home that night, we drove in silence, exhausted both mentally and physically from the events of the past few days. As we got close to home, our dark and unlit house seemed lonely, cold, and uninviting. This was in sharp contrast to the surrounding houses, which were warm and happy and sparkled brilliantly with various Christmas lights and decorations.

We all got out of the car in silence, and slowly walked up the driveway towards the front door. I turned to look at Lauren's house. To my surprise, she was at the window—her palm pressed against the glass as if reaching out to say hello. I acknowledged her by raising my arm slightly and pressing my hand against an imaginary window. Then I turned away and entered my house. I waited on the inside steps for my father to come in, hoping to make eye contact with him. He walked right past me and headed into the downstairs den. I slowly walked upstairs.

I helped my mother get David and Jackie to bed, then decided to take a shower. The water felt good and I stood there for a long time, trying to wash away the events of the past few days. It didn't work.

After drying off and putting on some clothes, I noticed that my dad had not yet come upstairs. Worried, I went to my mother. She was in her bedroom, turning down the bed.

"Mom?"

"Yes, sweetie?"

"Mom, I'm scared."

"Scared? Why, honey?" She motioned for me to come closer.

"Dad looks so sad, Mom." I sat beside her. "I feel so bad for him. I don't know what to do."

She put her arm around me, knowing that there really weren't any words that could make me feel better.

"I know sweetie; your father *is* very sad. He loved Rich very much, just like you love your brother and your sister. There really isn't much anyone can do for him right now. Just be there in case he needs you, okay?"

"Why did Uncle Rich die?" I asked in anguish, and rested my head on her shoulder. "Why did he have to die, Mom?"

"I don't know Michael. I don't know."

# Chapter 33

# Help Me Father

I LEFT MY MOTHER'S ROOM WITHOUT AN ANSWER TO MY question.

I went to bed.

"*Why?*"

I tossed that one little word over and over again in my mind. Maybe if I thought about it long enough, I would find the answer. Nothing came.

But I did not stop asking. "*Why? Why did he have to die?*"

I turned to God and said out loud to Him, "Dear Father, please help me understand all of this. Please tell me why this happened." But still no answer came. I finally put my head on the pillow and closed my eyes.

While I was trying to fall asleep, Dad was downstairs in the den, pacing slowly back and forth. The TV was showing the classic Christmas movie '*It's a Wonderful Life,*' but he wasn't watching it. Instead, he was asking himself the same questions I was: "Why? Why did he have to die?"

He finally sat down from exhaustion, just as George Bailey was pleading: "God...Dear Father in Heaven, I'm not a praying man, but if you're up there and you can hear me, show me the way. I'm at the end of my rope. Show me the way, God."

Suddenly, convinced that those words had been spoken just for him, Dad fell to his knees. "God, our Father, please help me ... I'm lost. I need you to help me. I need you to grant me the wisdom to understand all of this. Please teach me to understand."

But understanding still did not come.

I was close to falling asleep when the sound of the front door opening startled me. I jumped out of bed and hurried to look out the front window. It had begun to snow lightly and I noticed my father walking down the street. I knew what I had to do. I rushed back to my room and quickly dressed. On the way out of the house, I grabbed a football and ran to the middle of the road to see how far Dad had gone. Then I jogged to him.

"Hey," I said, slightly out of breath.

"Hey kid," he said weakly.

We walked together for a while, in the middle of the night with only the street lamps lighting our path...neither saying a word.

I broke the silence first. "Dad, I'm sorry about Uncle Rich," I said nervously.

"I know Michael. But why? I just don't understand why? Why did this happen? I mean ... what was the reason? Why?" I was surprised. Not by the questions Dad was asking—I had asked them myself—but because I realized that he was looking to me for an answer. This was totally unexpected. This was bewildering. He was the one we all went to for help. He was the one we all went to for answers. He was the one who made all things right. And now he was asking me, his teenage son, for help. He was asking me to help him understand why his brother was dead.

I wanted to help him. I really did. I wanted to help myself. We both needed to know. I searched for an answer, a reason, but I couldn't think of anything. My mind was a blank. He needed an answer and I didn't have one. I turned to God one more time and pleaded, "Please...help us."

*And then I knew.*

"Dad, Uncle Rich was special; that's why he died on Christmas Day."

"What?" He looked at me, puzzled and surprised.

"Uncle Rich didn't die on December 24th. He didn't die on December 26th. He died on December 25th...Christmas Day, the holiest day of the year. The day Jesus was born. Uncle Rich was special! I mean Christmas is Jesus' birthday, right? So you have to figure that God wouldn't allow anyone to come to heaven on that day unless they were special."

Dad continued to listen as we walked on.

"Father Valenti always says that our reward for the life we lead is an invitation into heaven. God wouldn't give that invitation to just anyone on Christmas Day. Who could be more special than the people who die on Christmas? God wouldn't invite Uncle Rich unless he had a special plan for him."

We both stopped dead in our tracks, and I stood there, not sure of what to do and stunned by the words that had come out of my mouth. I had not thought of any of this before, but the whole concept made sense. It was as if someone had told me what to say.

Dad was dumbfounded. His mouth hung open as his mind processed what I had just told him. He felt a sudden upwelling of reverence and realized that, for the first time since Uncle Rich died, his heart did not feel so heavy. He thought back to the questions he'd asked God in the den, just a short while before, and realized that his questions had now been answered. He had asked God why and the answer had come from his own son.

My father smiled and hugged me tightly. The football fell to the ground. He kissed me, then laid his chin on top of my head and closed his eyes. When he opened them, he noticed the football in the snow. Letting me go, he reached down for the ball.

"How about a catch?" he smiled.

As I ran out for the pass, I yelled, "Biletnikoff goes deep."

# CHAPTER 34

# SUNDAY, JANUARY 1, 1978

FOUR DAYS AFTER UNCLE RICH'S FUNERAL, THE FAMILY was together again.

It was New Year's Day, 1978 and the Oakland Raiders were playing the Denver Broncos for the right to play in Super Bowl XII. It felt strange not to have Uncle Rich with us, and over the course of the game each of us looked for him. No one mentioned him but he consumed our thoughts. Tension permeated the room as we watched the game, but our reactions were greatly subdued compared to the previous week's game. It was going to be difficult to get over the loss and sadness we all felt.

The game ended with a Raider loss. I watched the Broncos celebrate their victory in front of their home crowd, and sadly realized that the Raiders' championship run was over. They would not get to defend their championship in the Super Bowl against the Dallas Cowboys. I was angry at the time. Looking back now, it made sense. The last game my uncle ever saw was a great game, and it was also the last great game for the Oakland Raiders.

Although the Raiders would go on to have more success as a franchise, *this* Raider team—*our* Raider team—would never be the same. The following season (1978), the Raiders did not qualify for the playoffs for only the second time in eleven years, and by 1980, John Madden and thirty-seven of the forty-nine players from the team that won Super Bowl XI, four years earlier, were gone. Madden retired, Ken Stabler was traded, and my favorite player, Fred Biletnikoff, retired after thirteen seasons.

While the Broncos celebrated, my father and uncles slowly and silently left the room. It was as if another death had occurred. I thought of Uncle Rich and the Raiders, and how they would forever be linked in my mind.

The last great moment for *those* Raiders (the last great play: The Ghost to the Post) was on December 24, 1977, the day before Christmas...the day before my uncle died.

# CHAPTER 35

# A FEW DAYS LATER

A FEW DAYS LATER I WAS HOME ALONE...AND I WAS restless. I tried reading. I tried watching TV. I tried studying. I tried taking a nap...but I couldn't concentrate on anything. Eventually, I found myself outside the front door in the cold, and began to walk with no destination in mind.

I passed the houses of friends and family, but did not want to see anyone so I didn't stop in. Before long, I found myself at Joe's Candy Store. I walked in quietly and grabbed a pack of Devil Dogs and a SunDew orange drink. I placed the items on the counter and Joe came out from behind the curtain. He spoke softly.

"Hey kid."

"Hi Joe. How much?"

Joe started to ring up the items, and then stopped suddenly. He grabbed the Devil Dogs and the drink, put them in a bag, and handed them to me.

"How much?" I asked again.

"Don't worry about it, kid."

It took me a moment to realize what he was doing, but when I did, I gave him a huge smile and thanked him, hoping that he knew how much I really appreciated it.

Before I reached the door to step out, Joe called out my name and I turned to face him.

"Sorry about your uncle, kid. He was a real nice guy."

I was moved by the gentleness and sorrow in his voice. I opened my mouth to speak, but words did not come out. All I could do was smile at him and nod my thanks. I left.

I continued my walk and thought about going to see Father Valenti, but the idea of actually talking with him about the events of the past few days was just too painful. I thought about going to see Aunt Connie or maybe spending some time with Lauren or John, but neither thought gave me any comfort. Then I turned the corner and I realized where I wanted and needed to be.

There, right in front of me, was the school. I climbed over the fence and stood motionless before the ladder. I eyed each step. I had never really taken notice of them before. They were just steps. Now they represented something: a way to get closer to Uncle Rich. I knew that if I could get higher, I would be closer to him.

I started to climb.

Each step up the ladder sparked a distinct memory related to Uncle Rich, and as I made my way to the top, I fooled myself into thinking that, if I could just get closer to him, maybe he would be there ... that this had all been just some awful dream and would all be over soon.

He wasn't there.

Although I knew that God had taken Uncle Rich because he was special, and that his death on Christmas Day served some higher purpose, I still felt pain and great sadness.

I missed him.

I walked over to the bench, sat down, and prayed. I prayed to God. I prayed that God would make the pain go away. I prayed that God would help me go on without one of the most important people in my life. I prayed for my father and Aunt Connie, hoping that their pain would fade over time. I sat there for a long time, alone with my thoughts and prayers and the time passed.

At first I didn't notice Lauren sitting beside me, but when something stirred next to me, and I turned around to see what it was, all I saw was her smile. I was glad that she was with me. We sat together in silence and held hands as we watched the sun set slowly before us.

As I think back now, the events of December 1977 were basically a microcosm of what life is like for all of us. That month was filled with the highest highs and lowest lows. If I have any regret, it's that it all went by so fast. I thought I would be thirteen forever, and that nothing would ever change. In my mind's eye, I can still see all of it...and I realize now that Uncle Rich *was* right. Life doesn't stand still for any of us. It doesn't let you step off and call time out. It continues whether you're ready to move on or not.

I understand why God took Uncle Rich from us and although the years have dulled the pain I felt during that time in my life, it still lingers. It probably always will. But I look back now with a deep appreciation of that time and an understanding that, although everything has changed, there is one thing that has not.

My memories never change. They are exactly as they were. They are forever and they are mine. They are still as fresh and as vivid in my mind as when they first happened. Maybe it was because I was thirteen. I don't know. What I do know is that I *can* still feel it and I *can* still smell it as if I was right there again…just like Uncle Rich said I would.

# CHAPTER 36

# TWENTY-FIVE YEARS LATER

IT IS CHRISTMAS EVE, 2002.

I gaze upward and admire the gently falling snow, and once again question the events of the day. My eyes shift back to my parents' house and my mind races back to that time, twenty-five years ago—to when this story really began.

I look up to the sky and whisper:

"Not again. Please God. Not again."

Twenty-five years have passed since The Ghost to the Post, and Uncle Rich's death. I'm married now with three children of my own; Emma (14), Olivia (12), and Matthew (10). Matthew loves the Oakland Raiders—as if he ever had a choice!

My life is good, but my family has recently received some unfortunate news. My father, who has always been healthy, was recently diagnosed with cardiomyopathy. This is a rare disease that attacks the muscles that surround the heart. Over time, the muscles deteriorate, and the heart cannot survive without them. There is no known cure. The only option for a patient with Dad's disease is to have a heart transplant. Dad is 63 years old—not exactly a prime candidate. Given his age, the chances that he would receive a donor were a long shot.

All that changed today. Today, Christmas Eve, my mother received a telephone call informing her that a donor had been located and that surgery was scheduled for tomorrow, December 25th.

Christmas Day.

After the initial euphoria, I called the doctor to confirm the details. He indicated that my father's chances of surviving the surgery, and the 'rehab' period that would follow, were slim and that it was not uncommon for a patient to die during surgery, even if the patient was younger. When I heard the word 'die', the first thing I thought of was Uncle Rich. I think of him often, but more so at Christmas time.

I look around me as I stand, leaning against a parked car, in front of my parents' home. It is a pretty Christmas Eve. The snow sparkles with the reflection of the Christmas lights on the surrounding houses.

The thought that my father may die soon weighs heavily on my mind. The possibility that my father may die on Christmas Day is agonizing. I struggle with the thought that it's an "honor" that God may take another special person in my family on Christmas Day, with the fact that someone I love so much may no longer be with me.

The front door of the house opens. A woman emerges. She has long brown hair, olive skin, and shining brown eyes. She smiles as she approaches me. It is a smile that I can't remember ever being without...a smile that comforts me, and after all these years, still makes my heart jump.

Yes, it's Lauren. She's thirty-eight now too, but looks as though she could still be in college. She hugs me and lays her head on my chest.

"You okay?" she asks softly.

"Yeah, I'm fine," I say, not very convincingly.

"C'mon. I know you too well. Talk to me."

I start to talk and then catch myself, stopping abruptly.

She grabs my hand. "Talk to me."

I hesitate but then lift my head. "Not Christmas Day ... Not again. It's not fair. The whole thing's not fair...Why us?" I look into her eyes. "Why us?"

"Michael, it's not just us. All families go through things like this."

"Not like this. Not two people on Christmas Day. It's not fair."

"Who says he's going to die? Why can't he beat it?"

"C'mon, Lauren, you heard the doctor."

"Yes, I did. I heard that he's got a chance. You heard ... what exactly?"

"There's a chance he won't make it."

"He's going to be fine, Michael. We need to be a bit more positive about this, okay? We have to have faith. God will take care of it."

She moves closer to me, brushes the snow off my forehead, and looks deeply into my eyes. "You know," she whispers, "no matter how many years we've been together, I can still see the little boy I fell in love with. I love you."

"I love you too." More than she will ever know.

Lauren's eyes shift to the corner at the top of the street. My eyes follow hers to the spot where we first kissed. It looks different now, the trees and rocks replaced by houses and cars. She grabs my hand and we walk slowly over to it.

"Do you remember?" she asks.

"Of course ... right here," I say, looking at the ground.

"I remember." She smiles warmly as her mind drifts back in time, and she begins: "It was Thursday evening, December 1st, at about 7:30. You were wearing a dungaree jacket over your basketball uniform and black sweatpants. You asked me a question, and I moved towards you. I grabbed your arms and when your lips touched mine, my whole body shook. Your lips were soft, and I felt as if we had done it a hundred times. It felt natural, almost like it was supposed to happen."

She points to the corner.

"I remember a car came around the corner and that's when we headed back to our houses. After I stepped onto the side walk in front of my house, I glanced backwards to look at you one more time and you turned to look back at me. When you smiled at me, I knew. I knew that we would always look for each other. I knew that we would always be together."

I'm shocked. After all these years, she remembers every detail...just like I do.

And she had known right then...just like I had.

She grabs my hand and we walk back. "Come inside," she says gently. "Have something to eat and spend some time with your father."

"Okay. Just give me a few more minutes."

# CHAPTER 37

# MATTHEW AND A MAN ...

THE SNOW HAS STOPPED FALLING. I LOOK AROUND AT the houses surrounding me, most of them holding some memory from my childhood, and reminisce ... but only briefly because I hear the front door open again. My ten-year-old son, Matthew, heads towards me with a football under his arm.

"Hi, Dad!"

"Hey, Matt."

"What are you doing out here?"

"Just thinking, kid."

"About Grandpa and his surgery?"

"Yes. I *have* been thinking about Grandpa."

"Yeah, I was thinking about it too, for a while." He flips the football up in the air.

"For a while? Not anymore?"

"Well, I'm not worried anymore," he says with conviction, and continues to toss the ball.

"You're not worried anymore? How come?"

"Because I prayed to God and now I know he'll be all right."

The conversation turns from amusement to curiosity, as I begin to wonder what Matt is trying to say. "Oh yeah? How's that?"

Matthew looks directly at me and lets the football fall to the ground. "Well, remember a few weeks ago you told us that Grandpa was sick and that he might need surgery, but that he had to wait for a new heart…and that even if he had the transplant operation he might still not make it?"

"Yes." I'm getting more curious every moment.

"Well, that night, Mom told me to make sure that I prayed for Grandpa every night, and I did that for a week."

"For a week?"

"Yes."

"Why only a week?"

"Because then I knew he would be okay."

"How did you know?" I ask, starting to get annoyed with his quick answers. "How did you know?"

"Someone told me."

"Who told you, Matt?"

"I don't know. A man told me in my dream. I prayed to God right before I went to bed, and when I woke up I wasn't worried about Grandpa anymore. I felt happy, and I had, like, a poem in my head."

I'm not following him. "A poem?"

"Yeah. It just stayed in my head all day. It went something like: 'Today will end; tomorrow will come; the sun will shine, and everything will be okay.'"

The Christmas lights around me disappear. The chill of the cold December night is gone. I can't even feel my feet on the ground. My mind is reeling, but my entire body is numb and I cannot feel or hear anything for a long moment.

After what seems like an eternity, I compose myself. Softly, with an urgency in my voice, I ask the question I'm almost afraid to have answered. "Matt...where did you hear that?"

"I told you. I heard it in my dream. Someone told me it."

"But you don't know who?"

"No Dad, I don't. A man. I only heard his voice."

"And it came from your dream?"

"Yes."

For a moment, I return to the lake where Uncle Rich told me those very same words, twenty-five years ago. And now I'm sure.

For the last few weeks, my dad has been the central focus of my daily prayers to God. I have prayed furiously. I've prayed to God for my father's good health; I've prayed that God would grant him a little more time to be with us, and I've prayed for God to give me a sign that Dad would be okay. I've prayed for him, and I've prayed for me, and I've prayed for my family. I've prayed for my prayer to be answered.

And now it is. Now I know.

God has given me the sign I asked Him for. God has answered my prayer...through my son, Matthew, and through my Uncle Rich. Suddenly, my concern for my father begins to fade away, and I fully realize that not only is God a part of Matt's life but that Uncle Rich is now a part of it too.

I look down at the football on the ground and realize that it has begun to snow again. I pause and look up to watch it fall, admiring its gracefulness. Tears roll down my face as I am overcome by the enormity of this moment. It feels good to cry. It's as if the tears hold all the pain, anguish, and uncertainty I have been feeling these last few weeks, and as I wipe them away, peace and contentment fall over me.

I know I am not alone. Uncle Rich is with me. For a split second I can feel him...almost touch him. I know I am not alone.

*God* is with me. I can feel him ... almost touch him.

I know I am not alone.

I look up towards the snow-filled sky and whisper, "Thank you."

My son pulls on my coat and brings me back, "Hey Dad, you okay?"

I kneel down in front of him and hug him, "I love you, Matt."

"I love you too, Dad. You feel better?"

"I feel great! Now, how about a catch?"

"Yeah!" he replies enthusiastically, and starts to run down the street.

I pick up the football, brushing off the snow. Before I toss it, I feel a huge grin spread across my face...and call out to him:

"Hey, Biletnikoff!"

# Postscript

Dad survived the surgery—just like Uncle Rich said he would.

The doctors indicated that his rehab would take some time and that my mom needed to learn how to cook "like normal people".

As fate would have it, three weeks later the Oakland Raiders defeated the Tennessee Titans for the AFC Championship and advanced to the Super Bowl for the first time in 18 years.

I'd like to tell you that they won the game. They didn't. It didn't matter.

Matthew and I, and our entire family, watched the Super Bowl at my father's house as he recovered from the surgery. Matt got to see his Raiders team go to the Super Bowl, and more importantly, he got to watch the game with his dad, his grandfather, his uncle, and his great-uncles.

It was during the Super Bowl that I had another revelation. It wasn't the Raiders that made the games so special. It wasn't the winning or losing. What made the games special were the people that surrounded us, the people we watched the games with, and the moments we shared together. It was special because we loved each other and we cared for each other. The Raiders, the games ... they were important, but I know now that it was just a reason to be together: a reason to laugh, a reason to love, and a reason to remember.

To remember that we were a family.

To remember that life wasn't perfect, but it was enough.

I've known two great men in my lifetime. From them I learned many things. Most importantly, I learned that life is a precious gift and that only a foolish man takes his life for granted.

When I think of my uncle, I think back to my first baseball game at Yankee stadium, crabbing and fishing in the summer, and the love that we had for each other. When I remember him, I always remember December 24, 1977, and The Ghost to the Post.

When I think of my father, I think about playing catch on warm summer afternoons, watching football on Sundays, and how much he influenced my life. I'll always know that I received more love than any son ever had the right to ask for.

When I think of God, our Father, I know that He hears all of our prayers, and that His answers to those prayers can come from anywhere or anyone—even a ten-year-old boy.

And when I look at my son, Matthew... I know that my Uncle Rich is with him, and that all the people I've ever loved are... only a prayer away.

THE END